Breaking
Spirit
Bridge

Ruth Perkinson

Spinsters Ink
2008

Spinsters Ink
P.O. Box 242
Midway, Florida 32343

Printed in the United States of America on acid-free paper
First Edition

Editor: Katherine V. Forrest
Cover designer: LA Callaghan

ISBN-10: 1-883523-95-8
ISBN-13: 978-1-883523-95-4

*For my mother, Sue Perkinson, and my father, Gordon Perkinson—
because their journey became my journey.
I am honored to give them this.*

About the Author

Ruth Perkinson lives in Richmond, Virginia, with her dog, River. You can visit them both at www.ruthperkinson.net and also find out more about her first two books: *Vera's Still Point* and *Piper's Someday*.

Chapter 1

They were very sad when I died. I was very sad when I died. I did not die a natural death. Worse. I died a bipolar death.

When my brain caught fire the fall of my first semester at Blue Ridge University, I was sure it was my scriptural and metaphoric calling from all the Saints and Jesus Christ himself to save the world or at least fix part of it. After all, his spirit had come into me and my dog, Someday, and they told me in their mysterious ways that my brain was an allegory for the world. I had to look up allegory as I was confused on its meaning. It has the word "all" in it. Yes, I felt the *all* of something. It also had the word "gory" in it. I was feeling gory especially when I pictured my brain. It was like a weird Edgar Allan Poe story except it was *The Tell-Tale Brain*. Nestled inside my bony cranium were the ventricles, the tentacles, the veiny channels, the spongy gray rivulets of eggy moist caverns. Ahhh—eggy! They were my caverns and caves of lost and found and of stem and root and bark and flesh and of the viscous slick of blood and oil—the center of my bliss, the center of my darkness. This bulbous, gray tumor inside me held tiny loaded guns shooting thoughts like a *ra-ta-ta-tah* through the filaments, firing a million times a second. It hurt to think because it was like pieces of flint clapping together. The atoms, the molecules and the cells filled with the dark mental fluid that swept their cilia back and forth and shit inside my head. The black was my evil. The blue was my good. These colors swathed themselves in tendrils across the line of my vision making real and unreal suffuse together like an ocean raining up waves into the blue sky. Waves of blue in the sky. A sky with waves of blue, blue, blue.

I covered my mouth for fear I had yelled these words aloud and looked down at the spiral notebook on my lap. My penchant for yelling had escalated lately. Then, I thumbed a picture of me and my dog taken outside my cottage home in Banff, Alberta, the day I left Canada to come to Charlottesville, Virginia. Evidently, the center of the universe.

My world was upside fucking down.

Everyone I wanted was dead.

Closing my eyes, I thought of my dog. It calmed me. Looking down to my lap, I wrote her name in block letters—SOMEDAY—and then drew a picture of the wooded fort in Richmond, Virginia where I'd spent the first twelve years of my life. Holding the blue ink pen firmly to the notebook where I was sitting in a wheelchair with jeans and my basketball T-shirt on, I scrawled a picture of two large rocks, some plywood walls and a makeshift floor that held carpeting and an assortment of magazines and books and a walking stick. I drew Someday lying on the ground next to me. Her short, dark blond and chocolate hair, her rabbit ears and her short right-front midget paw that hung a good four to five inches shorter than her other ones. My dog walked on three legs and her name came from how my mother described that we would one day, someday get a dog. She had said "someday" for what seemed like sixteen billion years before a deformed looking puppy limped up to all of us one day while we were fishing near my fort. My father said, "Well, someday has arrived." The name stuck because we all laughed and it fit her kind of cool like because we found her on a Sunday, too. Kind of rhymey—so, Someday it was. She was my good girl.

The lights dimmed in the sterile-smelling hallway that led to the seclusion area of the hospital. Two nurses were behind plate windows talking to one another and writing on clipboards. One resembled Shirley MacLaine with her red hair and austere nose and pursed lips. The other was a heavier set woman with dark olive skin. She listened to the redhead while she told a story with her hands. They laughed and drank out of Styrofoam coffee cups. Three patients buzzed around each other from beyond the walled glass in the background. Two were talking to the air and one was picking at his dreadlocks and staring into the distance and rocking in place. A man wheeling up trays for dinner looked like he was tired from a hundred years of service and no one noticing him. He repositioned some trays and his white coat was a stark contrast to his dark skin. He was a skinny man, old and wrinkled.

"Evening," he said to me and tipped his head downward. "Chilly out there but the stars are out and the town just lit the holiday tree. Good news, eh? What's ya drawin' there?"

"My dog and my old fort." I stared at the picture and did not look back up to him. He edged over to peer at my work. I was a crappy drawer.

"I see you got a pretty BRU shirt on. You play ball?"

"Yes, I do. My dog is the mascot."

"Well that's something. I hear BRU women's basketball is having a good start this year?"

"Yeah. Have you seen my notebooks, though? I brought in my backpack here I thought."

"No, honey. I just do the food. I don't mess with personal belongings. I hope you feel better. You hear? My name is Jackson."

When I looked into his eyes, they turned to crosses. Perfect crosses, like in the vestibule of any church, but tiny, black crosses. My stomach dropped and I looked back down. He rolled his cart away. What the f dot com, I thought. Nothing made sense. More symbols. Just what I needed—but I wrote his name down anyway and his eyes and the crosses and the date in my notebook.

Tonight, I was missing some notebooks. I was hoping my room-mate, Teeter Mulligan, would bring them to me.

The truly unreal part was when my mom showed up shadowy and suddenly from behind and wheeled me into the seclusion area of Blue Ridge Medical Center. I saw two things. My grandmother who had been dead for seventeen years. *Flash.* No time to write that one down, my ride was too bumpy. She was in a wheelchair, too. We waved at each other. The second thing I saw was surely Satan's apos-tle, a criminal released from Petersburg FCI. He had on baggy jeans and was unkempt and his beard darkened his face as the X's appeared in his eyes. Surely, he had been released to stop me and the straw-berry blond girl, who was sitting at the table flipping through Uno cards, from completing what the people (who were wearing blue) were telling me through their third eyes. Quickly, I flipped through my notes to see. There it was. Yes! My notes had not failed me yet. *There's a snake in Brazil. A big one. Its venom will cure paralysis. If you contact Christopher Reeve, he will help. He has visions, too.* Got it. How the hell do you get to Christopher Reeve? I spat on the ground to get the evil away. My molars had a steady supply of spit. I spit-tooyed it out with a hiss. I sprayed the bad shit with it. I put spit-shine into everything. *Puh-tooh.* It shot out of my eye teeth like my own curi-ous venom. It scared the whack out of my mother who now parked my naked ass near the conference room. I looked around for signs of the snake. It was a big mother. And it was coming here, to stop my sorry ass from getting to Christopher Reeve. Maybe I should sum-mon Jesus. Around my wheelchair just outside the doorway behind the plate glass window, I spat an entire drooling arc and then stood up and put my hands in the air.

"Jesus! I'm calling you from about ten thousand miles away!" I shot my eyes from side to side and then snarled at the nameless crim-inal. He snarled back. "If you can hear me Jesus. I need Superman's phone number. Or, perhaps you can send Mary down and she can help me make the call. However you want to do it . . ."

Everyone, including the two nurses behind the window, was now staring my way. Good, an audience. Just what I'd been asking for.

"Shut up," the criminal yelled.

I spat on the ground again. "Son of a bitch," I barked back then spat again.

"Shut up!" He laughed out loud and then twiddled his hair. He was at the center of the corresponding room and there were two round tables and a TV hooked at the top of the far corner. *Entertainment Tonight* was flashing different movie stars and I could hear a bit about Robin Williams and rehab but then the news anchor's face turned into a feathery monster drenched in dark blood, so I looked back at the criminal.

"You're not going to touch that girl," I said to him, stepping on my arc of spit. "You leave her alone. You understand?"

Opening my notebook, I drew two stick figures in the woods. Then another picture of my dog next to the stick figure that represented me. The other stick figure had a Budweiser can in his large paw. I scratched his face out and turned the page. Inhaling deeply, I smelled the smell hospitals emanate. Dinner was being served to patients down the foyer past the large conference room and there was a sterile odor of bed sheets commingled with Clorox, the lingering smell of latex.

The criminal got up and walked away. The young, handsome freckle-faced girl playing Uno glanced at me. I nodded. Before I could get to Jesus, I sat back in my chair. Mom was gone. I could not remember how I'd gotten here. My palms were sweaty and my basketball shirt was soaked in sweat. There was a small bench with magazines on it. Further down the hall was an Exit sign. It was black and red—evil colors. The hallway lit up with incandescent spiraling arcs of glowing crystalline sound waves. I could see the speed of sound. Interesting. Perhaps Jesus or Mary were on their way? I hoped so. I was tired of this place already and that nameless criminal was going to try and hurt Uno girl and I was surely going to need all the saints, dead and alive, to manage this catastrophe. I barked out suddenly like I had adult-onset Tourette's syndrome.

"Send in Joan of Arc, too!"

"Piper?" A very swarthy woman came from around the doorway where I was making my stand.

Blue eyes. Good. There was a dark mole near her lower lip I wanted to touch. The mole grew a bit bigger, but when I looked away then looked back it was small and normal again. Real and unreal. I wasn't sure of the difference.

"Yes," I said and looked at her third eye, a piece of small, chipped charcoal in the middle of her forehead. Oblong-shaped. Real.

"Piper. Who are you talking to?"

"Evidently, you," I said and smiled. The mole was still tricky. Now it was breathing.

"I'm Paige . . . your nurse . . . who's going to check you into this unit. Do you know where you are?"

"Yes. Do you?" I opened up my spiral notebook and started to write down her name. Paige. I pressed hard into the notebook. P-A-I-G-E. From the E, I connected the top of the letter to a crude map of the United States I had already drawn. PaigE. The letters shot up into the air. I grabbed the P and the G through the crystalline sound waves and put them back down where they belonged. A sonnet. Ten beats per line. Beats. Fourteen lines. Fourteen. There will be fourteen prophets. Holy shit. Shakespeare was right. I scribbled madly. Iambic pentameter. Pentameter. Pentacles. Spirits. Holy spirits. I scribbled madly. I had to get the map right.

Write it, Piper. Write it. Then a loud clanging.

"Your friend here says you need some help and I don't think we can get any of the Kennedys here that you wrote down here as potential contacts. I think they're tied up in Congress . . . or in some other national matters, perhaps. Looks like at least two of them aren't even around anymore. Okay?" She smiled at me. "Is there someone back in Richmond who can act as your guardian, or help?" She looked up and behind me. I glanced at the Exit sign. There she was: Blue Ridge University's beautiful basketball star—my on-again, off-again girlfriend, Mandy Weaver.

Dark and statuesque, she sauntered up to me with her basketball sweats on and her basketball jacket. All in blue.

"Where's Mom?" I asked her as she sidled up next to Paige.

"Piper. Your mom is dead. Nearly ten years. Do you feel like she's here?" She shrugged, then examined the back of her fingernails and thrust her pinky in her mouth to have a chew. Her face distorted itself but I glanced down to my notebook to stop it. Then without warning, the Tourette's came alive.

"You have the universe traced all over your body as a reflection of the solar system, Mandy," I said, then looked at the nurse. "Your belly button is like the north star and then from there—"

"She has an aunt in Richmond and a grandfather who's in the VA hospital. He's been really sick though. Her foster parents are in Canada. They're the ones who really should be contacted. Her roommate, Teeter Mulligan, might have that information. I'll try and get her."

"Okay." The nurse made a note on her clipboard. "We'll wait for that; however, if Piper is to stay, then she will have to check herself in."

"She's a student at Blue Ridge University on basketball scholarship. We just had our tournament opener at John Paul Jones arena and there was quite the incident there."

"The EMTs who brought her in gave me that information. Sounds like we had quite the evening out, eh, Piper?"

Quite the evening. Shut up. I rolled back slightly and did not respond. Instead, through the conference room window, I watched the trees waving in the darkened December sky and put my hands to my head and covered my eyes. In my head I said, *That's the Spirit.*

Mandy slumped down in a chair, and crammed her hands into her warm-up jacket. She sighed then began the unveiling I couldn't stop. "She's been talking about great novels and the book she's written and how Nelson Mandela created some kind of wheel that needs to be ridden by the Pope. It's her womanifesto."

The Uno girl gazed at me from the conference room table and waved. I waved back. I gave her the peace sign. She giggled and gave one back.

"Do you have this with you? This—what?" Paige asked with a

raised eyebrow.

"She calls it her womanifesto," she whispered.

"I can hear you," I said.

Mandy went on. "All I can see is that she's filled notebooks full of phrases and words and pictures and diagrams and none of it makes any sense."

Dadaism. That's what I wanted to say but knew that neither one would understand the nonsensical reference akin to the cool song by the Police, "Da-do-do-do Da-da-da-dah." This was freakin' related. Come on people; connect the dots.

I gazed at the greasy red-headed girl playing Uno, then noticed a man enter the sitting room beyond the bulletproof glass. His skin was pitch black. He must have been kin to Buddha. If Shrek had been black, this guy was it. Giggling internally, I smoothed my hair back to wait for the next sign.

Then it came.

The magazine on the bench whispered to me. *Over here, Piper. Over here. We've got a message for you.* I looked at Uno girl who nodded to me. Another sign. Then a spiraling arc of thinly veiled glass floated in my line of vision, I pushed my sweaty body, still filmy from tournament play, toward it. I reached out, feeling tiny pinballs rotate beneath my index finger. Mapping the arc in perfect circles with my fingers, I felt the same circling vibration in between my legs, in my stomach, in my breastplate. Joan must be on her way. Good. I hoped she had that golden white horse. The gauntlet of saints was ready for her re-approach. Writing down Joan's name would be important. So, I did: blue ink, only in my notebook.

Getting up from the womanifesto inquisition, I walked over to the magazine that wouldn't shut up. Quickly, I grabbed it and then the dirty dread-headed criminal sat down on the couch near me.

Mandy glanced my way. "Hey, can you come back over so we can talk."

She was agitated and Paige appeared to be watching my every move. She scratched her mole and I thought I might jump out of my skin.

"What's your name?" he asked. "Here, have a seat." He patted the couch.

I reeled back a bit, unsteady, and then sat. "Piper."

Paige glared at the crusty criminal beside me and sighed, "Come on. Leave her alone. We have some work to do." She turned to Mandy and they began a series of Dadaisms that I couldn't make out. Words were garbled. Mandy talked with her hands. Paige's eyes danced.

"Give me your hand, Piper," he said. He smelled like alley dust.

"Why?"

"I won't hurt you." He slithered his tongue at me. Then something between my legs contracted in a weird, unexpected way.

Tentatively, palm up, I gave my hand to him.

He grabbed my forearm and yanked me close. "Now, why don't you put this down my pants, Piper?"

No one heard what he said but me. "No."

"Why?"

"Because I don't want to!"

He laughed like a Manson maniac, dropped my arm, then got up and walked away.

As I opened the magazine, my eyes saw the flashes of light mapping between the Greek keys, and then the labyrinth, and then that jungle in Brazil I needed to tell Christopher Reeve about. Through the twelve point Helvetica font surfaced the message: *Happy Birthday, Piper. We're glad you're back. Watch for the palms by your bed.* I looked both ways then slapped the magazine shut and spat on the floor. Both criminals, black Shrek and the smelly dreadlock man, were at the table with Uno girl.

Sensing my confusion, Mandy came over and sat down next to me. She looked pinched and worried.

"Piper. I'm going to call Vera and Jenny and Andrea to see if one of them can come and help. I'm not sure what to do, Piper. You're in trouble and you need to sign yourself in. Do you understand me?"

Mandy held the clipboard and showed me some more lettering. It was a maze of black and white symbols and it all ran together like black blood. Looking again for my mother somewhere in the foyer and not finding her. I put my hands back over my head and eyes. Nor did I see dead Dad. Nor did I see dead Jack, my brother. I longed to, though—longed to see them all.

"Piper. What do you see?"

"Nothing," I said.

"This nurse—I'm sorry—what's your name?"

The nurse sat down next to us. I was in the middle. I did not want their faces to change, so I looked to the floor . . .

"Paige. I will be her nurse on this floor if she signs in."

"I don't know sign language," I said.

"Piper, you don't have to know sign language to get into this place." Mandy laughed nervously, then looked at her watch.

Paige crossed her legs. I crossed mine exactly the same way.

"You don't need to be a Pantomime, either. Jesus." Mandy's lips looked suddenly like worms. I looked away and into Paige's blue eyes. Blue is good. Then I slicked my hair back and into a ponytail, pulled my baseball cap from my back pocket and adjusted the back band annealing the Velcro just so. I put my hand up and noticed from the corner of my eye a man disguised as a doctor. A white coat overlapped a curious dark brown shirt. I pulled the ponytail through the cap and pulled the brim down low over my head. We made eye contact and his pupils changed to crosses. I looked down again. This time hoping the floor wouldn't change. Spitting was necessary but I held it back.

"Who's that?" I pointed.

"Doctor Spectrus," Paige said then finished scratching her pen across the medical array of paper.

Standing at the corner of the nurse's station by the bulletproof glass, Dr. Spectrus sported khaki pants and a full belly over the belt of his pants, the buttons tight on his white coat. His hair was long and frizzy from the sweat beading on his forehead. He pushed his gigantic Mr. Magoo glasses up his nose and his face seemed red and splotchy from too many Scotches in the afternoon and evening. He scratched notes down like a mad scientist. His shoelaces were half tied and he held in a burp and then let it out gently through his nostrils that looked wide and African, even though he was Jewish.

"Happy Hannukah! Hannukah!" I yelled at him. "Go Menorrah!" I yelled.

"Piper—are you going to sign the papers or not? I gotta go. Okay? I have a huge makeup exam on Monday. Can we get this moving along? We've been here for two hours." Mandy's jaw dropped open.

"Is it in English? Do you need some help?" On that, Mandy got up and walked away.

Paige put her hand on my forearm. "You okay?"

"He's Jewish, right?" She did not respond. I looked down at the floor. "I'm just exhausted. I feel like I haven't slept in twenty years."

"How old are you?" she asked.

"Almost twenty. My birthday is December twenty-fourth."

"Well, that's certainly a long time not to sleep. Your eyes seem older than twenty." She smiled and then took her hand away. "We'll make sure you get some sleep here. But you are going to have to sign this paper before we can admit you." She lifted it for me to sign. Then came the black ink pen.

I took it from her and pressed my hand and the tip to the paper. *Happy Birthday, Piper*. The page sounded itself. The Exit sign glowed, and the Uno girl flipped cards. The TV in the lounge had a police chase ensuing. It scared me. Confusion laid its dark, mushy face on everything.

"What's wrong Piper?"

"Do you have a blue ink pen?"

"Yeah," she said. "Hang on, I'll get one."

My lips quivered and my breastplate was heavy. Where Joan was I didn't know but I wanted her to hurry. *All my saints, God, all my saints*. I needed them all because what was getting ready to happen was going to kill me for sure. I looked for a spired arc in the air, a dot to touch, a dot to connect. Then my head turned up to the ceiling and there it was: the portal to heaven. What the fuck dot com. Here we go again. I wanted to shed my skin because the snake was in me and with my rapacious nature, I was ready to expunge that one. That demon. *A long time coming you son of a bitch*. I spat on the deep dark floor and curled my lips into a snarl. The shoelaces on my sneakers suddenly turned into tarantulas and with my screaming, "You son of a bitch!" over and over again, I cleared the floor of people in a matter of seconds. My heart beat all the way through my iron breastplate in my chest. My heart, my heart, my heart, like the letters in the air were outside of my body. I tried to reach out to put it back in. To put it back in . . . back in, back in.

It took six men to hold me down while Paige screamed at my grandmother (or what I thought was my grandmother) to get to her room. Like a sailor on crack, I bellowed out every cuss word that wanted to tunnel up and out from my bone marrow. Everyone and thing was suddenly a mother fucker and a son of a bitch and the two dark criminals were cock-sucking dickless snakes and they better not touch that pretty girl or I would kill them both. Kill them both. Both! Both! Both! Kill the pedophiles and rapists. All of them needed to go. Motherfuckin' time had come for that one. I spat all over everyone and the drool came down my face. I was one to be reckoned with and Joan was on her way so get the fuck out of the way of fuck.

They put me in lockdown. I lay on a white bed and signed a piece of paper with blue ink. I told Paige who gave me some water in a Dixie cup to never forget this. She said she was sure she wouldn't. I asked where Mandy was. Gone. She was gone. I wanted her here next to me. I tilted my head and looked out the barred window. I longed for something from deep within my limitless inner sanctum but did not know what it was. Paige made some notes on a chart and told me to rest a while. I said that I was tired.

"Well, you've told me how tired you are. No sleep in nearly twenty years will make anyone tired. Makes me tired just thinking about it. You'll get some rest here. Just relax. I'm going to bring you something to help you sleep that Dr. Spectrus prescribed." She walked out and returned shortly with some pills in a small paper cup.

"What is it?"

"Lithium, Depakote, Risperdal and some Valium." She placed them in my outstretched palm. Her third eye was so delicate in the middle of her forehead and I trusted her blue eyes.

"Paige?" I asked.

"Yes?"

"Thank you for holding my hand. Thank you . . ." I said, shakily.

The clanging started from next door, and then the scuffling, and then the yelling.

"What's that noise?" I swallowed the pills.

"What noise, sweetie?"

She didn't hear what I was hearing. I shut up to keep my secret. If I let any more out then she would think I was really crazy. Christopher Reeve needed to be contacted soon. If he couldn't be summoned then the snake that was coming through the vent up above would make it into my room. I looked at Paige. Her hair stood up at the top and I moved it around with my eyes. The clanging got louder and the room became blood red. I was scared of that viper and now my only hope was walking out the door.

For fifteen minutes I lay there scared, confused, and then a little voice inside my head told me to wet the bed. So, I did.

Chapter 2

Coach Vanessa Potter yelled her controlled yell: "I want Jessie, Natalie and Mandy down on the baseline running through this next drill. Move. Get there. Then I want Kara and Piper in the one and two spot feeding them the ball back and forth rapid fire. Orange team pick up defense on any one of them. This is a shooting drill people. Mix up your pivoting and shoot from instinct. Move. Get there." We all moved like scared ants.

Potter was one of the most seasoned coaches in NCAA Division I basketball. At forty, she'd seen over eighteen seasons at Blue Ridge University, taking the program from sixteen people sitting in the stands to a packed house by winning two ACC titles and going to the sweet sixteen the last eight out of ten seasons. Her nemesis was Debbie Ryan across town at the prestigious UVA. The hometown rivalry was one of the biggest in the state of Virginia and in the ACC conference.

Potter had a presence like I'd never seen, plus she was a hottie. Her auburn hair was shoulder-length and her cheekbones high and her eyebrows, arched from years of plucking, framed her large blue eyes like a perfectly pieced mosaic. I could barely look at her without feeling quirky inside. None of us could.

Nerves vibrated through the hot field house where we lifted weights, tried Yoga for meditative purposes, and then waited for her to show up and bark at us for nearly three hours. School, schmool— this was basketball and it was taken as seriously as all the other men's and women's sports combined. She yelled and we moved—even if it was to run to get water. Fast. Fast. Fast. The whole town of Charlottesville either loved BRU or UVA and the competitiveness ran deep like the Rivanna River.

Preseason practice started the second week in September as I was just getting used to finding the route between my apartment on campus, my classes in the humanities building and the gym. Charlottesville, Virginia, was a long way from my home in Banff, Alberta, where I'd spent the last six years of my life safely away from my neurotic grandfather who lived in Richmond. He'd reluctantly given me up to my foster parents when I was nearly thirteen and he ended up not caring much about anything except beer, NASCAR and his friend Clover who tried to molest me in the woods one hot summer night. Luckily, my dog bit his sorry ass so bad that he didn't get too far.

Someday lives with me and my roommate, Teeter Mulligan, on campus. They allowed Someday to come to BRU with me and my basketball scholarship on account of the fact I wouldn't come without her. When a dog saves your life, you understand the meaning of loyalty. Potter even asked the athletic department if Someday could be our home game mascot since we were the Blue Ridge University Mountain Dogs. Someday wasn't much of a mountain dog, but one of the team mothers made her a vest and as long as she would sit with the athletic trainers at the end of the bench, the athletic department was okay with it. Potter told me to bring her to the practices to get her used to the noise, so I did. She hung out near the water cooler and was a good girl.

"Mandy, do three ball fakes before you pass it back up to Piper. At least three." Coach Potter went up to Someday and patted her on the head. "Good, Piper, you do the same. We're working the right side only right now. Get used to each other. Use your eyes." Someday licked her lips and looked at me. I caught her gaze then looked back at Potter.

My stomach dropped with the new nerves of this foreign place. Then I ball-faked to the right down low and then pushed the ball to the right up high in the hot gym air. Sweating through every orifice possible, even the lids of my eyes were beaded up, the salty drops pinged onto the court. My breath was ragged and short and spasmodic. I went to the left up high and then put the ball almost on my right hip and then catapulted it to Mandy's outstretched arms on the block of the baseline. *Phhhht.* She reached for it before Saneha Jones could wipe it from the air. Mandy pivoted around and faced the basket. I stepped into the open spot waiting for the ball to come back to me. When she passed it back, I shot. The ball arced through the air. *Swoosh.* Right through.

"Good, Piper. Nice shot," Coach Potter said.

"Thanks," I said, placing my hands through my dark wavy hair and eyeing Mandy.

"It wasn't *that* good. Do it again. This time Saneha, close up that passing lane better, girl. Get the lead out of your feet. You need to move faster than that or you'll be riding the pine and getting splinters through winter session."

We did it again. Saneha was pissed. I could see it in her face but she didn't say anything. Just tried harder. We ball-faked the right side till coach told us to move it to the left. She told us that just because the ball was on the left side didn't mean we could lounge around on the right and inspect our cuticles. I giggled and covertly observed Mandy. She glanced at me sideways then looked away. My legs felt melty.

Mandy Weaver must have been six feet two and her thick straight black hair was sweaty slick to her head. Her slender nose was perfectly straight and her eyes were mud brown. She had no freckles, but one small mole on the corner of her cheek. A beauty mark. She looked like a dark Meryl Streep but she carried ten extra pounds, maybe fifteen. It was her midsection that carried it . . . everywhere else, she was pure muscle. A senior at BRU, she was a just-miss All-American from what they wrote about her: the silent one who had the most versatility of any other player on the team. She was a four spot; a shooting forward. I was a three spot; a shooting guard. I was a good three inches shorter and was rail thin even though I could eat a trillion times a day. Andrea and Jenny, my foster parents, called me hyperactive and claimed they were glad I was finally going off to college so the grocery bill would be less than the mortgage. I was hungry every twenty minutes. Vera, my guardian who lived with us back home, said to eat all I wanted whenever, as long as my nose was stuck in a book. I did what she said.

We continued the drill till I thought my hands would go numb from catching the ball. Mandy and I created a good rhythm on the right side and then we switched sides to balance it out. Shooting the ball close to fifteen times, I made nine of them fall through. Coach told me I had to do better than that. I thought it wasn't bad but made a mental note that I needed to practice more from outside of the three-point line. From baseline extended, Mandy and Natalie worked their magic. I was the freshman, they were the seniors and knew the syncopation of good basketball moves. When Saneha hopped into my position, I took a break and watched from the perimeter next to the young and handsome Scott DuPont, the assistant coach. I liked him because he asked us to call him Scott and to call him anytime we needed anything. He gave us his phone number, e-mail and home address the first fifteen minutes of my first day on campus. I liked him right away. He hung out with Someday on the sideline and gave her a bowl to drink from. An all-around affable man, he was married to the assistant dean of admissions.

"When you shoot the ball, Piper—" He looked at me and whispered, "Get it a little off your shoulder and more above your head. Just a thought. When you're farther out, you compensate because you're having to shoot farther out. Weights, girl. You gotta hit the weights and beef up those shoulders of yours."

"Thanks. Duly noted," I said and drank a cup of Gatorade handed to me by Kissie the manager. Weights. Hit the weights. I repeated it in my head to remember. From the distance, I could hear the campus church's bell tolling, striking five times to indicate the time. I counted along with it.

Coach Potter yelled at Teeter Mulligan, my crazy roommate, to shoot the ball. I'd met Teeter right away when I came to BRU and liked her because she was always cussing and drinking and telling people what she thought. A local girl from near Culpeper, she was the first black girl I'd really hung out with, ever. Teeter didn't really like Coach Potter but she kept her lips shut because she told me the scholarship was her ticket to the world. Teeter drained two consecutive shots and then did her funny groove thing I'd never seen anyone do after they shot. She put both hands in the air like she'd scored a touchdown and then waved her hands back and forth. It cracked me up. Teeter looked at me and I gave her the peace sign. She put her index finger to her head and twirled it around her temple to tell me I was a crazy ass as she'd recently begun calling me.

"All right, ladies! That's enough!" Coach Potter barked at us. "Everyone on the line. It's time to run. Coach DuPont, take the lead. I'm going to watch. If anyone throws up, we run some more."

We ran suicides in reverse.

"Touch the last line first," Coach Potter yelled, "then do the three-quarter foul line, then half-court, then this foul line." She pointed then blew the whistle. We ran like scared soldiers all thinking the same thing: *I don't want to throw up.* Saneha was in the lead, then Natalie, then me. I was fast but not as fast as them. I tried to keep up but my lungs compressed and Jessie Holmstead, another freshman from Rockville, Maryland, passed me on the half-court line coming back. The rest of the team sounded like a herd of cows lumbering hard from behind like a bull run. They were all big and large and I wasn't sure how the blood got to their heads. Everyone's shoes were squeaking as we hit each line and bounded back and forth. When the first suicide was over, we all put our hands on our legs and hovered over the freshly stained wood in Pierce's Field House.

"Good ladies. One down. Twenty to go. Come on, now. That's the spirit." Coach Potter drank her Gatorade and smiled, somewhat deviously. Internally, I hated her suddenly but liked her all at the same time. The way a coach wins respect, I guess. Break them down and then build them up. Break down; build up. Someday sat up and watched us, especially me. On one quick break between runs, I darted over to Someday and kissed her between her eyes and shook her midget paw.

On the tenth suicide, Saneha threw up in the trashcan. Coach told her to suck it up and get back on the line. Mandy glared at her with a twinge of disdain, then raised her hand.

"Coach?" Mandy asked breathing heavy and uncertain. It was the first time I'd heard her speak all week. Suddenly, I was nervous and scared for her at the same time.

"What do you want, Weaver?" Coach Potter retorted.

"Coach, I'll run Saneha's suicides after we're done." She looked right at Coach Potter.

"You'll run Saneha's suicides for her?" Coach Potter answered rhetorically.

"Yes, ma'am."

"Saneha, you hear that? Mandy says she wants to run your suicides for you. What do you think?"

Saneha had her back turned to coach and said, "I don't care. She can run 'em if she wants to." On that Saneha sat down. The problem player, I had heard.

"Stand up, Saneha," Coach Potter said. She did so, but slowly. "Kissie, get some water for her. Saneha and the rest of you basketball wannabes, I have one thing to tell you before this season gets underway. No one runs for anyone else. You got that? This is a team that takes the hit all the way around. If one player is hurt or sick, then everyone picks up the slack. I hope you can take Mandy Weaver's lead here because she just earned all of Saneha's extra suicides, but not because Saneha threw up, but because Saneha said she didn't care. If you don't care then I don't want you on my team. I don't care who you are and how good you are. A team is a team. Period. Everyone together as one all the time not just some of the time or caring some of the time. Got it?"

"Yes," we all mumbled in unison.

"Got it?" she asked louder and rotated her head to take in all of us.

"Yes, ma'am!" we yelled.

"Let me hear it again," she yelled.

"*Yes ma'am!*" This time it came from our stomachs and we meant it.

"Good. Now back on the line. We have an hour of running."

After the last suicide was finished, three players had thrown up, and I was dizzier than I'd ever been. My legs were liquid and my insides buzzed from the pounding of the wood floors. Coach Potter finished her end-of-practice talk and told us all to have a great weekend and that Monday would be just like today. We all looked at each other in quiet dismay. My body would be pureed by the end of September.

Natalie Wingfield, who was from Santa Barbara, California, and who had a surfer body and bleach blond hair smacked my butt with a towel as we headed for the locker room. It scared me and I turned to look.

Saneha laughed at my pinched reaction. "What's wrong, Canada? You can't take a smack on the ass?" She twiddled her nappy dreads and then rolled her towel and laid one on Natalie.

"Ow. Saneha, I'm going to choke your brown neck till you want to smack your Momma." Natalie put the towel around Saneha's neck and they started a mid-air wrestle that caught the eye of Coach Du-Pont.

"Cut it out, you two," he yelled from across the court. They stopped. I looked at Mandy Weaver and she rolled her eyes at me. She smiled. I followed her footsteps all the way back to the locker room. Someday limped along behind me but I was sure my gait was worse than her three-legged one.

The locker room had two wooden benches down the middle and

eight rows of lockers for all of the female athletes at BRU. The fresh-men all had bottom lockers and Coach DuPont had given Someday one right next to mine. I kept her vest, some dog food, two plastic bowls and a water bottle that had her name on it. Teeter Mulligan had her locker next to mine since she was assigned as both my room-mate and mentor.

"Piper, you have a funny name and so does your dog," she said, smiling at me and pulling off her sweat-stained shirt. "How you got the university to allow dat dog in here is beyond me. She's a stinky dog, but not as stinky as you."

"Teeter, you're dumb," I said and sat down on the bench to pet my dog and unlace my shoes. "And what's with scoring a touchdown in the air every time you make a shot?" Lockers were opening and closing and people were gulping from their respective water bottles.

"Dat's my sign. My signature, goof. Everyone has one, right you all?" Teeter sat down on the bench and patted Someday tentatively on the head. "When you make a hoop, you throw your hands in the air cuz it feels good . . . all the way down to my toes."

"Yeah. And she's always the first one back on defense when she makes a shot. That's how she gets most of her playing time. By the way, who's having the opening ping party tonight?" Theonia Huff-man asked as she pulled a hooded sweatshirt over her head. She was large and butch, her hair was shaved close to her head. A junior cen-ter from where I did not know.

Teeter stared at her. "Theonia, what's wrong wif you? Are you cold? What the hell you puttin' on a sweatshirt for? It's a thousand degrees in here."

"Ping? What's ping?" I asked nervously then looked down.

"Ohhhhh. Piper you just earned your freshmanly duty!" Nikki Jackson, a senior from New York, pointed at me. She flashed her brown eyes at me and giggled. Then everyone stared in my direc-tion.

"What's that?" I asked. My stomach fell. They were pinning something on me.

Kissie was sorting through hot towels and folding them near the laundry room. "We got to break the freshman in!"

Break me in? This did not sound good.

Mandy Weaver slicked her hair back and then closed her locker. "Well, you all have fun. I'm going back to shoot free throws."

"Don't listen to Weaver, Piper. She's an overachiever who makes the rest of us look bad," said Kara Featherstone, the one-guard transfer from Penn State who was an All-American her sophomore year. She said this and pulled her shorts off.

I looked away from her muscled legs and looked at Mandy. She was looking right at me. "How many are you going to shoot?" I asked.

"Oh, no, you didn't." Saneha put her hands on her hips. "Piper, you can't go shoot with Mandy. You got some errands to run before we all show up at your house for the ping party."

"What's ping?" I asked again. No one wanted to pay attention to the question.

"We're going to need a case of Mickey's Malt," Kissie the manager chimed in. "What's wrong with you, girl? Get a pen out of your backpack. You need to take notes." She eyed Teeter and they both laughed.

"I guess I'm it," I said. I reached into my bag and looked for my favorite blue pen. Got it.

"Ping, you're it!" Mandy pointed at me and laughed and walked out.

Evidently, each year a freshman was "pinged" to have the opening basketball party after the opening week of preseason. My stomach was in my heels and I was very quiet and resigned, looking for something or someone to give.

Teeter got up and came over and sat down on the bench next to me near my locker. Teeter Mulligan was number twelve coming off the bench—the player in last position. Coach Potter only put her in when she wanted to enliven the others because Teeter was a hard-worker: a walk-on who'd earned a tuition scholarship. Her touch-down-wave thing after she scored had become something fans and players looked for and loved. She smiled her toothy smile. "You're going to need some help with this list . . . and we need to get a ping pong ball."

"A ping pong ball?" I asked.

Kara turned from pulling her shirt over her head. "We're playing pong, goofy. You ever hear of pong in Canada?"

"No."

"It's a drinking game and you'll laugh your ass off. Although, you don't have much of an ass to laugh off." She shut her locker and walked out. "See you guys later." Everyone grunted good-bye. Paulie, Katherine and Jamaica were all lying on the floor still sick from the running. They were freshmen like me. From Kissie's pile of towels, I grabbed a bundle and threw them over to them. Paulie and Katherine high-fived me and Jamaica grabbed my hand and held on to it. It seemed odd for a moment and then I just let go.

When I walked through the doors to cross the gym, I saw Mandy Weaver shooting free throws at a side basket with Coach DuPont. She shot while he fed her the ball. Commitment, I thought. She did it the same way each time. Three dribbles. Slight knee bend. Then a pause to take in the basket and a slow, methodic shot. I watched her make four out of four then I left with Teeter to go get beer and a ping-pong ball.

"Who's going to come to this thing tonight?" I asked Teeter as she got into my black Toyota pickup truck, a hand-me-down gift from Jenny on my birthday last year when I got the scholarship to BRU. Unclipping Someday's leash, I lifted her up into the club cab. I kissed her between her eyes and the church bell began a tolling of six times.

"Everyone. The whole team."

"Do we need to get decorations?" I hopped in and tossed Someday's leash into the back.

"Hell no, girl. This is your first party at BRU's big house. We gotta move some furniture out of the way and put some plastic on the floor. Someday probably should stay up in your room till everyone either pukes or passes out. Kissie scared a dogs anyway. It's going to be fun girl. I'm glad you spoke up as the dumbass freshman who doesn't know anything. I think Paulie and Jamaica saw it coming. I'm not sure about Katherine. She might be a dumbass, too."

"Teeter, shut *your* dumbass," I flashed back and smiled.

She smiled back. "You're a funky girl, Piper. Both you and your dog have funky ass names, too."

"You're the one with the funky ass name—Teeter."

"Well it's better than my real name," she said.

"What's that?"

"You don't want to know—it's gay."

"You have a gay name?" I asked.

"Portia Contessa Mulligan."

"What's wrong with that? It's very Shakespearean. Cool."

"Shakespeare is gay. That's what I mean." She laughed and put her hand to her mouth. She got a good cackle going.

"I'm gay," I said.

"No shit, Piper. I knew that the minute I met you."

"Are you gay?"

"No, just my name. I like dick."

"Is anyone else on the team gay? Who's dick?"

"Shut up! Theonia is and Natalie is and, oh, Mandy Weaver is. I think we're about fifty-fifty on this team. Most teams are about that way . . . usually more gay than straight, I think."

"I pegged Theonia and Natalie, but wasn't sure about Mandy. She's hot."

"Yeah, she's a heartbreaker, too, from what I hear. At least one girl from the lacrosse team left school last winter because of her. I think Mandy started seeing someone else on her and the girl just broke down."

"You're kidding?"

"No. People break down sometimes over losing someone you love. Mandy's a looker. I think she knows it, too. And with that, you're going in." She said this as I pulled into the nearby Giant. The light of the September day was beginning to fade upon the mountains. The horizon shimmered with heat. I jumped out then reached for my wallet from the console.

Teeter pushed her seat back and stretched her legs out the window. Dangling her flip-flops, she said, "Get me a pack of Slim Jims, four bags of the chip variety, and make sure you get some Cheetos. Make sure you get four cases of beer. Oh, no, Theonia can drink a case by herself. Make it five cases of beer. Oh, and cups. We need plastic cups." She twiddled her wig on the side and looked in the back at my dog. "Get Someday some rawhides, too. We gotta keep our mascot happy."

"Teeter, your hair looks like you stuck your finger in a socket. You want me to get you something from the black girl hair aisle?"

She gave me the finger.

"Why am I the one getting all of this?" I asked.

"Because you were pinged and you're a stupid gay freshman! Now leave my cute wig out of this and get your lazy ass in there and get the stuff. We've got furniture to move before the basketball cavalry shows up. They can smell beer from Walton's Mountain around here. People around here are crazy about that namby-pamby show still. Cracks my crack ass up."

"You're a lazy ass with your gay name, Portia Contessa. What are you royalty from Culpeper, Virginia?" I turned on my sneakers and headed in.

Teeter yelled at me. "Don't call me Portia in front of these people or I'll smack your momma, Piper!"

"That's okay, she's dead."

It hurt to say this so flippantly about my mother who died when I was nearly ten along with my father and brother—boom! All at the same time, in a crossroads, an intersection where my drunk grandfather ran a red light drinking from his can of beer, I'm sure. The pain still channeled through me like a continual current I couldn't move away from. Clanging and jolting sometimes against my thin frame, my thin heart. God and Jesus had a lot of explaining to do; I had told Vera this once when we were eating breakfast on a Saturday. She told me that good dialogue was helpful but sometimes yelling was the most appropriate.

I missed Vera's sardonic funny ways. The old retired librarian from Louisa County, Vera was my guardian who looked like a butch gnome, but cuter. I missed Jenny and her wacky humor and Andrea's flapjacks. Jenny was long and veiny and tall and strong—a handsome woman. She taught me every basketball move I knew and helped me earn a scholarship. Jenny delivered mail in Banff and was like a good friend, a good buddy. Andrea was more like my mother. Her hair was strawberry blond and shoulder-length. She was thinner than Jenny and had English features: a slender, short nose; high cheekbones; and smooth, white velvety skin you wanted to run the back of your hand across. Andrea was book-smart. Jenny was street-smart. And Vera was just Vera. They had risked everything to get me away from a life of being raised by my neglectful, abusive, alcoholic grandfather.

Now, as I walked into the Giant and tried to find my way through the aisles of chips and soda and beer, I became confused as if all the labels were yelling their ingredients out at me and I had to read it all before moving along. My body was numb from the strenuous exercise, and now the whole BRU team was coming to my and Teeter's apartment down by Union Hall and the Monroe Park footbridge where I walked Someday each morning to where the steam would rise like the breath of saints from the low mountains like it did in Banff.

Strange. I felt strange here in Virginia, only an hour away from where my whole family had died in Richmond. By September in Canada, we already had snow and I could hike up Tunnel Mountain with Someday all morning and not think of anything at all. Vacant. My mind would stay vacant as if the cool wind could rush through my ears and nothing, not even a brain, would stop its flow. Brainless, thoughtless, vapid, vacant. Bliss it was, walking with my dog by my side: one of my favorite activities. Driving to BRU in late August was fun, too. Someday's head out the window and ears flapping in the wind was bliss, too. Together, mapping out the road signs and finding our way together. Jenny and Andrea had insisted that they would drive the gazillion miles; but I told them I wanted to do it alone.

Vera told them to let me. So, they did.

Chapter 3

"Move that piece of carpeting next to the sliding glass doors, Piper. And, get your dog upstairs. Truck number one just pulled up and we still need to get plastic on the floor." Teeter barked orders at me and I obliged.

We iced down all the beer in three different coolers outside. Teeter clicked her iPod into the docking station and put Usher on full blast. I tuned my Fender guitar in the unlikely case I needed to fill in and then I ran Someday upstairs to my room and put food and water down for her. Kissie Martin had come early to help and she was putting chips in bowls and lighting candles and getting the beer bong put together.

The front door opened and the mixture of voices entered saying "hey" and "yo" and "whassup."

"Yo, get in here! Who needs a beer? Y'all help yourselves to the ones on the patio. Natalie, help me with this plastic. Piper is upstairs fixin' her curly wig and can't get herself down here." Teeter turned up the music and I could hear the low roar of the train of women entering our small campus apartment.

Quickly, I put on a black T-shirt that said Dogs Rule and then managed to bust a sag with my khaki cargo pants and some black flip flops. I sprayed perfume on my neck and Someday jumped on my bed. I kissed her head and her ears and went to the doorway. "I'll be back to get you in a while to sing you a song. Okay?" She stared at me with slight discontent as if I were jailing her for the evening. "Okay. I'm coming back in a little while with a bone. Does that help?" She whined that that was good and I shut the door and hurried down the steps.

The room had a beanbag chair, a long oblong coffee table from Ikea and a bubba chair. A couple of guys from the men's team came in I found out quickly Ping was a stupid beer drinking game. You formed teams, and then a large cup full of beer was stationed at one end of the table and people took turns with a ping-pong ball tossing it to see if they could land it in the cup. If you made it, then you got to tell someone from the other team to drink. It was the drinking game akin to basketball.

"Teeter, you want to be on my team?" I asked taking a large gulp of beer and watching Mandy Weaver enter the party. I eyed her all the way in and Teeter smacked me in the back of the head.

"Kissie, you want to be on Piper's team? I can't. She's too gay." Everyone looked at me.

"I sing John Denver songs." I shrugged.

"That's really gay." Mandy was now next to me telling me so. She was wearing a tight red shirt and her jeans were flared at the bottom. Her toenails were painted purple and in some wedge-like shoes I did not recognize as something you might buy from Dick's Sporting Goods. The place where I got all my clothes.

"Want to be on my team?" I asked.

She looked at me, kindly, I thought. "Aren't I already on your team?"

"For Christ's sake? Who wants to play with my gay roommate?"

Teeter put her hands in the air and everyone laughed. The music got louder and the vibration felt good.

I laughed. "I think you are thinking of two teams: the gay team and the basketball team. Right?"

Mandy took a long sip of her beer. She had on mascara and eye shadow and a hint of red lipstick. It made me weak but I drank in unison with her. "I thought you were looking for a partner for the ping team?"

"Will you be my partner? I promise not to sing John Denver and if I make this tiny ball into the cup, I'm sure I'll make a big splash with you . . ."

"Oh, God, shut up, Piper!" Kissie and Teeter and Natalie all said this almost at the same time.

Then, like it was some kind of religious ceremony or something, most of the BRU players put on sunglasses. I asked Teeter what they were doing and she said it was some sort of bonding tradition they'd been doing since her freshman year. "We're radonkulous!" Her word for ridiculous—she liked it because it sounded more like it should. I told her it sounded like a farm animal. She told me to shut up and then hit my butt with her large strong one. She nearly knocked me into Mandy but at that point, I didn't care. The attraction had already welled up inside my tiny chest.

The tossing of the tiny ball into the cup began. The front door stayed open and there was a steady influx of people I knew and didn't know. Natalie "the surfer" Wingfield partnered with Kissie and for a while they pinged everyone at the party.

"Yo, Piper, dude—what's all this stuff you've got written down over here? Is this your diary?" Natalie held up one of my notebooks.

"It's my journal. Give it here . . ." I opened my arms.

"I want to read it. Can I?"

"No. It's private . . ." But she opened to the middle of the notebook. I broke away from Mandy who was next up at a go at the beer bong and leapt over the beanbag chair to get to Natalie.

"What's wrong? We're a team. We can't hold anything back from one another." She and Kissie laughed.

Kissie sipped from a straw that was swirly, twirly like a snake and said, "Yeah, we need to learn each other's weaknesses before we can play with each other on the court."

"You're not a player. And give it here, Natalie."

She laughed and held it over her head. She opened it and began to read from one of the entries. "Up Route Twenty, there's a special bend in the road that should be traveled by all who are on the journey of life. It is a bend like no other because it points to what we need to see. The spirit of the trees, the spirit of the animals (especially horses), the spirit of the land and the bridge linked from this world to eternity. It takes all travelers from all walks of life: white, black, Jewish, Muslim, Indian, Islamic, Catholic, Hindu, Wiccan—"

Everyone laughed.

"—Buddhist, criminals, jailers, doctors, nurses, lawyers, gay, straight, handicapped, autistic—animals of all kinds, especially dogs who were given to humanity from God as a gift to learn how to be human in the first place—"

Teeter grabbed it from Natalie. "That's enough, you radonkulous ass. This is Piper's stuff."

"I like it. I was only getting to know our star three-spot from Canada a little better . . . sorry, Piper."

I wanted to run away. Teeter handed me the notebook and I whisked myself upstairs to my room and landed on my bed next to my dog. She whined a bit and I patted her on the head. Picking up my guitar, I placed a cold cup of beer next to my thigh and strummed a few chords. Andrea had made me choose an instrument and after seeing them watch Melissa Etheridge a thousand times on DVD, I'd picked the guitar. Three years of practice and I knew a small arsenal of songs.

Mandy Weaver appeared at my door five minutes into my solo of "Sweet Surrender" by John Denver.

"What is that?"

"One of the gay songs I know." I stopped playing. "You're having fun with the stupidest game on earth and then the great orator Natalie Wingfield as a surprise guest reader."

"Wingfield didn't mean any harm . . . can I sit?"

"Come on Someday, move up a bit." She moaned but obliged.

Mandy sat and crossed her legs. "She just thinks it's funny to make fun of people. She's really a good egg and would probably do anything you asked her to do."

"Like evaporate?"

"It was sweet."

"What?" I asked.

"What you wrote. It was sweet. I liked it. You're a good writer. Better than me. I can barely stop a sentence with a period much less figure out where to put a comma."

"When in doubt, leave it out," I said putting my guitar on the floor.

"Leave what out?"

"The comma. When in doubt, leave it out. My friend Vera taught school for a while and knows all the rules. She made me learn three times more than what the school taught us. She's strict like that but funny and kind of charismatic."

Just then, Jessie Holmstead peeked into my room. "You guys finished playing ping? Or are you going to have multicultural night up here with Piper the singer and writer."

"Shut up, Jessie!" I said. "We're coming down."

Blue Ridge University was a smaller school than the more well-known University of Virginia but it, too, was one of the most serene, elegant universities in the world. Founded by Jefferson's forebears, it had a long-standing vision of bringing together philosophers, scientists, mathematicians, artists, writers from around the globe. It was my secret dream to be among them—to be a writer who had some kind of greatness to send out into the universe. I felt at home to be in the mix of such formidable thinkers and artisans. To walk across the campus and see the Greek architecture and the way it was cradled by the green of the Blue Ridge Mountains. It was sensuous to me—smelling the wind that carried the variegated energy and thoughts of the thousands who had walked the lonesome stony paths and had fingered the mortar and mud and bricks that made the facades come alive with the romance of history and yearning and longing. Spirits. The great spirits of humanity right in Virginia. People who had changed the world forever by letting the golden channel of light flow down from the heavens and through them out into the paralyzed thinking of the tedious masses. It was all so pastoral and bucolic and like one of those coffee table books you see in rich people's homes. Over the skyline, one could make out the rolling hills of the Blue Ridge splayed with pines, bare oblong stretches of rich, green land. The air seemed denser here and the Virginia breezes were sweet and slow and melodic. The hundred-year-old oak trees flexed their brawny branches and their rough outer core longed for touch, it seemed to me. Two minutes out of town up Route 20 where I'd taken my dog, you could see three- and four-board fences neatly nailed together and painted dark brown and a pristine white. The old split rails broke the pattern every few miles. A mélange of horses stood on the hills next to the sheltering oaks and kept their heads to the ground, their teeth snapping bits of grass and earth. Cattle farms and dairy farms and goat farms—Charlottesville was a mecca in the middle of a country coffee table book.

By the middle of September, I'd discovered that I loved to wander around, especially driving with my dog. At least three days out of the week, Someday and I would drive all over the place looking for road signs and drinking beer. I'd put on a pair of cargo shorts, a loose white V-neck shirt, some flip-flops then buy a six-pack at the Giant and some treats and water for her and we'd go for several hours at a time. By the time I returned to Teeter and whatever beauty routine she was in, I'd be drunk and ready to drink some more.

Finding Miller Lite was the sexiest thing around besides the mountains I whizzed around. After our ping party, I was recognized as one who could hold the most beer and not seem drunk. Theonia had held that high accolade, but I drank her under the table by nearly three beers. She spent the night at my place and the next day said, "Piper, I've never seen such a skinny person drink more than that. Is it because it's so cold in Canada? Did you do nothing but drink up there?" I told her I had a natural tolerance, she told me to shut up.

Driving settled me down in the same way that walking Someday did or even dribbling the basketball and shooting did. The hum and the repetition of the wheels along the paved roads and the whoop whoop whoop of the wind through the cracked windows were like rocking to me. The arc of the ball; the dip in the road—opposite in their cadence but they filled in the yin and yang of my soul. The beat of the basketball coupled with the beat of the road assuaged the thoughts that sometimes swirled in my head. My mind resounded like a buzzing cicada song in summer; starting with a low buzzing and then sometimes getting so noisy with thought that I would jump in my truck and drive to clear the clutter. My head was jammed up.

My coming to Charlottesville, and at night, it had gotten worse because I could rarely sleep. I would lie down and then the rat on the wheel would start to spin the thoughts in my head. It might begin with imagining a rudimentary piece of summer grass and then, suddenly, I was out the window of my room, then up on the roof, then to the coast of Brazil and the harbor there where there was drug trafficking and then to Africa where I talked to Nelson Mandela about apartheid and had he ever read that poem I wrote for him. Then I laid in his jail for twenty years and watched the bugs and the loneliness and the jailers walk about with food, day in and day out. I floated to 1945 and wanted to untie the twins that had been sewn together in a Nazi experiment. Picking up Virginia Woolf, I asked if I could stay in her room even if it was for only one night. I kissed her. She put her tongue in my mouth soft and slow. We held hands walking to her river and I told her that the planes overhead weren't that bad and could she just put some earplugs in because we wanted her around a little longer. Alongside Woolf, I stopped and asked Marlowe if Shakespeare is a fraud and he showed me a large snake around his neck and a chalice filled with beer. We got drunk and talked in iambic pentameter. He mounted me and slid his penis inside of me, I gripped it with my contracting vagina.

I stopped and looked at the clock. Forty minutes since I closed my eyes and this waking dream began. I called for Someday to come close to the bed and then made her hop up on it. I patted her head and kissed her between her eyes. Her fur felt warm and smooth against my lips. She whined a bit when she rolled on her side and exhaled. Then I drifted to sleep for a few hours till Marlowe wanted to talk again about how he thought Will had taken his writing. Altered states—in my head, in my heart, in my soul and across the whole world without end.

The third week of school and many restless nights later, I found myself sitting near the humanities building where I was taking Freshmen English. Reading from the syllabus, I gladly noted that I'd read all of the books less one—*The Awakening* by Kate Chopin. Someday was curled up next to me and I put some water in a plastic dish by her side. Writing down a list of things to do, I suddenly and frenetically turned to writing some notes and thoughts I'd been mulling over the night before. Express. Express. Express. Then the clanging just about sent me over the damn edge of the brick wall I was sitting on. I stopped then looked up, then thought some more. Think. Jefferson was a thinker. Franklin was a thinker. *Think, Piper, think.*

Two girls walked by with iPods in their ears. They both stopped to pet Someday—they barely noticed me but that was okay.

"She's cute," the first girl said.

"What kind is she?" the second girl asked.

"She's a shepherd-rabbit mix," I said. "Her ears look like a rabbit's ears; hence, the descriptor."

They giggled and walked away. "She's BRU's mascot for women's basketball. You should come to the games to see her next month," I yelled after them but they didn't hear. *That's the spirit.* Someday put her paw on me and I patted her head. I kissed her in between her eyes and told her she was a good girl.

I was free for the first time in my life on this campus. Nineteen and free. But I continued to feel pathos, a longing for my foster parents back in Canada—Andrea Winter and Jenny Black. The third woman there was my official guardian, but mostly my friend: Vera

Curran. She had saved me in a different way than Jenny and Andrea had. Vera Curran was a transplant to Canada from Richmond, Virginia: the city where I'd lived the first twelve years of my life.

Vera was a rebel. A retired librarian from the Louisa County public school system who had seen what prejudice can do to people firsthand. She'd left Virginia for freedom in Canada. She said it was the best example of irony she'd ever witnessed in her life. All three had taken me to Canada to raise me to be gay, they would joke—when I actually turned out that way they all stared at me and said collectively, "Are you sure? You don't have to be. It's okay to be straight." I shrugged and told them it was the twenty-first century and gay people sometimes took themselves way too seriously. Vera barked at me, but her bark was always worse than her bite.

"What is it again? *The Awakening*? I can't hear you Piper. Speak up." Vera was on the other end of the phone.

"Yes, *The Awakening* by Kate Chopin. Have you read it?" I scratched Someday on the back of her ear and she licked my sweaty knee and whined in pleasure.

"A long time ago. It's good. You should read it. But don't waste your money on a copy. I think I have one here. I'll send it to you."

"Okay. Where are Jenny and Andrea?"

"Out running errands. You want me to tell them to call you? Everything okay with basketball? Have you met any nice people?"

"Basketball is good. We're into preseason training and everyone gets the willies when Coach Potter opens her mouth. She's cool though. She burped into a microphone the other day really loud and it cracked us all up. I like Teeter, my roommate. I feel like a snowflake in a coal mine though, every time her friends are over. I haven't really hung around black people, but I tell you Vera, they are funnier than white people. The way they talk to each other is like a whole other world of dialect and inflection. Freaking crazy," I giggled.

"You hooked on ebonic, girl?" Vera quipped.

"Ebonic is the only language I like right now. Forget Kate Chopin. These characters are something to witness. Teeter says, stuff like 'wuz wrong wif you grill gih, you need a dental plan. Can you say dental plan' and she's lookin' right at her best friend who has a gold tooth. They just bust on each other right in front of their faces. It's hysterical."

"Good. That's good. You needed to get out of your white ass element in Canada and get multicultural. That's good for you. Are you coming home for Thanksgiving or do you want to wait for Christmas?"

"I don't know yet. I need to see what practice is going to be like over the holidays. Christmas is looking better . . . we can celebrate big number twenty. I'm kind of embarrassed that I'm a nineteen-year-old freshman though."

"Well, I know, sweetie. That's okay. Just tell people you got held back on account of your move to Canada from Richmond. You don't have to tell them the whole story. This will satisfy them. It's okay to be nineteen and a freshman. How's your math class?"

"I dropped it," I quivered when I let this one out.

"Why?" she exhaled slowly.

"Because I walked into class and this man named Professor Givens had on a full suit and talked about statistics like it was the second coming of Jesus Christ."

"Good. Just don't tell Andrea and Jenny. You can pick up another math course next semester or in the summer session. And why the hell did you pick statistics as your freshman math? Isn't that a little high-level?"

"I placed into it. I scored the highest on my math placement test than anyone in my group."

"That's got to be the biggest miracle I've ever heard about. Remember how awful you were in math when you first got here?"

"Yeah, the days of puking over math tests are over. I'll take it next semester, but will probably take something not so taxing. Perhaps business math."

"Have you met any girls?"

"Just the ones on the team . . ." I paused. "We had a ping party after the first week of basketball preseason—"

Vera laughed. "What's a ping party?"

"A party with ping pong balls, beer bongs and Teeter Mulligan's iPod on full blast."

"Hmmm . . . is Jackie Rivers still calling you from here?" Vera asked.

"No, she stopped. I'm glad she finally got the message when I stopped returning her calls."

"Well, that's all for the best. I don't think she truly appreciated you for who you are."

"Maybe so. I don't know. I miss you guys so much . . ." I tested the waters. "I'm thinking about driving to Richmond to see Victor."

The answer was immediate and sharp. "I thought that bastard would have died by now." Vera loathed my grandfather for everything he'd done and hadn't done for me. She had waged her own verbal war against him for six years.

"He's at the veterans hospital in Richmond. Aunt Emma called . . . I thought she called you, too, Vera. Anyway, she said he was sick and he wanted to see me—"

"Piper?" Vera stopped me. "She did call. Where she was six years ago when that mess was happening, I don't know. I gave her your number but thought you would say 'Hell no!' to such a request. I just don't understand."

"He just asked. I don't know. I kind of want to see the old homestead, too."

"You mean that lurid, dismal apartment complex you lived in?"

"Yeah. I wouldn't mind seeing my old fort. It's only an hour from here. This place is beautiful—"

"Well, suit yourself. I'll get *The Awakening* in the mail to you. Are you going to tell Andrea and Jenny about your potential visit to Victor?"

"Can you?"

"I'll tell them. But don't ask me for anything else till Christmas. I love you. Make your shots and study hard."

"That's the spirit, Vera. Hey, one more thing."

"Yeah?"

"I'm writing some stuff. In a journal and some notebooks like you said I should do." I paused then looked at my dog. "Someday is getting old you know. I think she's having a hard time adjusting to the place. She's nearly twelve years old."

"Someday has got a lot of wear on her yet, Piper. Just keep loving her like you always have. I think I might miss her more than I miss you. Damn dog."

We hung up and I looked at the foyer in front of the science building and saw Mandy Weaver reading something from a textbook and taking notes. She was studying. I shoved my cell phone in my bag and decided I was up for a potential flirt with her. I went through my brainal archives to flesh out a possible discussion. Duh. Stupid. Talk about basketball. Cypress trees. No, basketball was better. Cypress trees? Where did that thought come from? Amalgamations of the greatest poets of all time. Start with William Blake then work your way up to Nikki Giovanni. No, she was at Virginia Tech. Hmm. Dogs. Talk about dogs. Come on, Someday. I put my hands through both sides of my hair and then tried to rub the freckles off my face. Lemons. No, don't talk about lemons.

I poured Someday's water out and clipped the leash to her collar. She hobbled with her three good legs, holding her bad leg to her side. Her back legs were arthritic, but her left front leg was a solid strong hobbler. I put on my sunglasses in accordance to the BRU basketball tradition and put both arms through my backpack and shifted it just so. Watching Mandy Weaver the entire way over to her was like looking at a piece of moving sculpture. The way she looked down and flipped through the pages, she exuded grace and elegance in her hard body. Interesting contrast.

"Come on, Someday," I said—she was walking slower than I wanted. "Let's go talk to this chick and see if I can get her to notice me. Come on, you're acting like you're paralyzed or something. No sniffing crotches, please." I leaned over and whispered in her ear and scratched her chest. Jelly. My stomach was pure jamming jelly.

Alongside Mandy was a line of buzzing students all doing the same thing—hovering over textbooks and reading papers and texting and chatting on cell phones. Someday slowed up and when I got near Mandy, she glanced my way.

"Hey, Piper." She waved. "Nice ping party the other day. Sorry again about Natalie."

"That's all right," I said. "Someday and I went over to her dorm the next morning. We crept in and I put on a Melissa Etheridge CD on the highest decibel I could find in her player. Then cranked up 'Somebody Bring Me Some Water' and put Someday's water bowl on her bed. When she catapulted out of the bed it went everywhere. I told her she was radonkulous."

"Then what happened?"

"We went and got coffee at Starbucks with Someday and sat outside in the sun. Wingfield is cool. She can dish it out, but we . . ." I patted Someday, "We can give it right back."

Mandy laughed. "You're pretty smart for a freshman."

"You're pretty smart for a senior."

Mandy put her notebook and pen down and closed her laptop. Then she reached down and patted my dog on her head and stroked her ears.

"What happened to her paw?"

"Birth defect, I guess. She came this way . . ."

"Where'd you get her?"

"Oh, no. She found me limping across a bridge near my home in Richmond when she was a pup. Just limped along and saw a bunch of goofy kids and decided she needed to be a part of our family."

"She decided . . . you're funny. I'm glad she's our official mascot." She paused and reshuffled some papers in her bag. "So, how do you like BRU women's basketball so far?"

"I like it. Coach Potter seems nice and I've always liked Coach Dupont. He's the one who recruited me. I told him I could only come if they let me bring Someday. He said it would be fine and it sealed the deal for me. I had no idea she'd become the mascot and get her own locker. I think Coach Potter has a weak spot for dogs."

"Potter is the best. I think she's one of the best coaches in the nation. She's not as well-known, but I think that's good in a way. I love playing for her. She made me into a much better player. Her house is cool—" Then she trailed off. "You've got quite the imagination, you know. I liked your Route 20 description the other night. Was all that just a figment of your imagination or do you really believe it?" Mandy stood up and leaned over to pet Someday more.

"Oh. I have a lot of figments. Pigments too." I touched my freckly face. "Speaking of figments and figs and pigments and pigs. Do you want to eat?" This suggestion came out much faster than I anticipated.

"Figs?"

"No, I mean, would you like to get some food or some coffee or a beer?"

"You got a fake ID?"

"Lord, who doesn't? I just haven't gotten around much and seeing since you're a senior and have been around some, perhaps you wouldn't mind showing what's cool about Charlottesville and Blue Ridge University. I know we aren't UVA and Debbie Ryan and all but we're just as loud and proud, right?"

Mandy stopped petting Someday and stood straight up. Someday lay down on the sidewalk with a *whumpff.* Mandy pulled her shirt over her midsection and smoothed it out on the sides. It was a long-sleeve BRU shirt that said Women's Basketball across the front. Her jeans were button-fly and I couldn't help but notice how she sucked in her stomach a bit when she tucked in her shirt. She slipped her feet into her flip-flops.

"You're very forward, Piper. For a freshman, you're kind of weird. I saw you scribbling in your notebooks in the locker room after practice yesterday. What are you studying that's so incredibly important?"

"Oh," I said, feeling a bit awkward, "it's nothing. Just some stuff I'm writing."

"Like the stuff from the other night or is it school stuff?"

"No. Just some poetry and some prose pieces that are compressed. A womanifesto, I think, not a manifesto."

"I have no idea what you mean by that. I'm no good in English or in writing. Science, no problem." She smiled and put on her Jackie-O sunglasses. Her black hair held her face like a square frame, strong and even on all sides.

Garnering a cup of courage, I decided to give her some shit. "So, Mandy, that's the most words I've heard you speak since meeting you on the basketball floor. Is speaking a problem, too, or is it just the readin' and writin'?"

She slapped me on the back of the head.

"Ow!" Someday barked. "Good girl. Bite her, Someday. Bite her!"

"Well, let's go to La Taza," she said. "It's a cool place not far from here and we can sit outside. I need to run a quick errand and make a call. Are these better words for you, freshman smartass?"

"Webster's is going to want to interview you for the twelfth edition coming out next year. You know parts of speech, too? How about etymology?"

"How about if you shut up and I meet you there?"

I liked her. She was smart and good-looking and seemed slightly unsure of herself. When she smiled at me it was like she couldn't look directly at me but away at something else. Sparky. I felt sparky. I wanted to throw my arms in the air like Teeter but thought that would be a bit much.

I looked over my left shoulder and noticed the oak trees waving in the wind, a cool breeze from the west blew my tendrils into my eyes. My knees suddenly started to quiver. "Direct my sail," I replied.

"Direct your sail?" Mandy asked. "You are crazy, Piper." She took off her sunglasses and put the ends in her mouth. I suddenly felt silky all over. She leaned over to get paper and pen from her backpack. I could not keep my eyes off her muscular body. The striations and veins in her forearms bulged from years of weights and sports. Her long fingers were sculpted in an elegant gradation, even and smooth. I longed to hold her hand.

"What's crazy about giving me directions, silly? Someday is smart but she's not good behind the wheel. I'll have to drive us both and I don't have a GPS."

"You're crazy, Piper."

"Smokin' yes I am." I patted my dog on the head and looked at the people on the right. Three men working the drainage system thirty yards away were wearing sunglasses and looking our way. It suddenly gave me the creeps. One looked right at me and I looked away. My stomach felt sick and my palms got hot and sweaty.

"You know those guys over there?" I asked.

"No, why?" she said as she scrawled out directions. I felt compelled to spit suddenly but held back.

"Nothing. They look like they're from Hollywood."

"Here you go." She handed me the directions to La Taza. "See you in about twenty minutes. I might call Kara to join us. She's doing some extra shooting practice with Natalie and Jessie but they should be done by now. She's been my roommate for my whole time here. Copasetic?" She pulled her glasses from her mouth and put them over the sultry eyes that for a quick second looked right into mine. Her pupils got small, pin like. Suddenly, I fingered the cross around my neck.

"Copasetic? Copasetic. Now that's a big word for the senior. See you there," I said.

"Just a little test, Piper. Your dog is really cute, by the way. I think I like her."

"Well, I can tell she doesn't like you. Be careful. She's been known to attack bad people at opportune times."

"Don't make me shiver!" she said and walked away.

Holy cow! Score! Someday! We scored. I could barely contain myself I was so happy. Mandy Weaver was hot and now we were going to meet at a restaurant and drink beer. Yee ha. Oh God! My hair. What did my hair look like? Did I look too butch with my Surefire Sparkplug T-shirt and shorts? She was femme away from the basketball court with her spaghetti strap top covered up by a long-sleeve T and bold leather belt and tight jeans.

I pulled up my shorts and tried to comb my crazy hair with my hands. I tapped on my cheeks to give them some color—a trick Andrea had told me once before I went on my first date.

Someday and I ran all the way to my truck. We stopped three times so she could catch her breath. Her back legs hurt her. I helped her in and turned on the engine. I gave her some water, pulled my notebook out of my bag, and began the first notes of my true womanifesto. My lucky blue ink pen scrawled the letters and words across the page till I had the essence right.

Then a little voice came from the back of my truck. *You have something to say. So, say it. The world wants to know.*

I looked at Someday and grabbed her paw to hold on. Then she licked me right in the mouth. Good girl.

Chapter 4

It took me forty-five minutes to find La Taza. Charlottesville's premier cartographer and road designer must have done blotter all the way through map school. It was a direction nightmare. I couldn't find anything. This route number branched off here and that route number ended there. I circled the area to find myself going around the downtown mall till I finally stopped and asked someone where the hell La Taza was and if Thomas Jefferson was so bright then why didn't he map the goddamned streets better.

Well, at least that's what I thought. My palms were sweaty as hell and I was more excited than I'd ever been. Mandy Weaver was cute and nice. Two things you rarely find in a girl. Easy to talk to, too. That bit about the womanifesto was radonkulous, my new word that I stole from Teeter. After twelve beers, Teeter would say, "That's just radonkulous, Piper. You see that Paris Hilton on TV. Ra-donk-u-lous. She giving Martha Stewart a run fo her money. Radonkulous."

It was a catchy word. I liked it.

When I pulled into La Taza, I saw Mandy sitting by herself. Good. More quality time.

The restaurant had tables both inside and out and it looked like a Mexican Cantina. Lucky—Mandy got a spot outside. The trees surrounding the place were lit up with brilliant reds, yellows, and oranges. The distant mountains were cloaked in a dark green velvet.

"Hey, how much beer can we drink and still make it through a preseason practice tomorrow?" I asked as I told Someday to lie down next to the red maple tree just behind where she sat.

"I don't know, Piper. You seemed to be able to drink everyone under that table at the ping party. Think you can handle a few here?" She smiled, her teeth even on the top, crooked and chipped on the bottom. Nice physical flaw, I thought.

"So, tell me about BRU basketball, anything I should know?" The waitress came over to me. "A top shelf margarita, please."

"You're going to puke in a trashcan tomorrow if you drink that."

"Okay, scratch that. I'll have a bottom shelf margarita." Mandy looked at me funny when I said this. "Okay, scratch my dog instead. I'll have a Miller Lite. Make it a double." Mandy just stared at me. "I drink fast, Weaver."

Mandy looked at the waitress who seemed slightly contemptuous of our small chatter. "I'll have a Corona Light, thank you." The waitress did not respond and walked away. "You're different, Piper. Where do you come from?"

"How much time do you have for that answer?" I winked at her, opened my bag, pulled out my cell phone and turned it off. "I don't want any interruptions for this radonkulous story."

She laughed hard and leaned forward. "I see you've been hanging around Teeter Mulligan too much. She's her own radonkulous self, now, isn't she?" We high-fived in a dumb basketball kind of way.

The waitress brought our beer and I downed the first one in about six minutes. Mandy Weaver was impressed with my drinking ability.

"You're a good shooter," Mandy said.

"What, with the beer?"

"No, with the basketball, goofy. When did you start playing?"

"Like everyone else, when I was a kid. But my foster parents, especially Jenny, she showed me how to shoot and dribble. We played with each other nearly every day for six years."

"Foster parents. What happened to your folks if you don't mind me asking?" She sipped her beer and leaned back in her chair and shifted her legs open.

"My mother and father and brother all died in a drunk driving accident when I was about ten years old. I had to stay back at home with Someday on account of the fact she was sick. My mom made me. Then my drunk grandfather got behind the wheel and killed them all six miles down the road. He walked away with stitches in his head."

"Jesus Christ, I'm so sorry." Mandy put her beer on the table and then reached over and put her hand on my hand. I wasn't expecting the show of grace. The stoic foul shooter had some heart. My knees quivered. I covered her hand with my other and then quickly released them and grabbed my beer.

"It's all right," I said.

"What do you mean, it's all right? God, how do you manage all those emotions? The loss? You seem so well . . . well-adjusted." She swallowed a large gulp and did not take her large, green eyes from me this time.

I glanced at the table next to me and felt peculiar again, the way I had felt on the lawn earlier when I saw the people in the sunglasses. "I don't know. I make sure Someday is okay and I pray sometimes." I was slightly embarrassed by the last comment but gulped the words down with my beer. I was beginning to feel the effects of the alcohol and I loved it.

"You pray?" she asked like she hadn't heard.

"No," I said, "I'm gay." I winked at her.

"Touché, me too. How long have you been out?"

"Since the embryonic stage. That was my first closet, but when I played basketball at my high school in Banff, Alberta, that was my first clue. I fell in love with a junior forward, Jackie Rivers. She threw me over last year for some girl she met in California on vacation. But sometimes she still calls. My foster parents are on the committee, too." I ordered another beer. "Can we get some nachos, too, please—"

"Your foster parents are gay?"

"Yep, they are the happiest, funniest, silliest gay people in the world. Their good friend, Vera, put us up in Canada when my grandfather gave me up to them. We've lived there ever since. The Canadian Rockies kick the Blue Ridge Mountains' ass, any day."

"Hey, now. I like these mountains."

"These are pussy mountains."

"You're a pussy, Piper."

"Makes you want to kiss me, doesn't it?" The buzz encircled my head and my flirt-o-meter had turned on.

"Oh, for God's sake, aren't you the flirt!" Mandy laughed in my face.

"I'm taking by your giggle that kissing is not a possibility. If this is the case then I will have to do what we Canadians do in order to keep our dignity."

"What's that? Are you going to embarrass me?"

"Me, embarrass you, the star basketball player at Blue Ridge University? Never."

"So, what do you do to regain your dignity?"

"We kiss someone else." I leaned over to the table next to me. There was an older couple, fifties I was guessing. The man was in a wheelchair and had on khaki pants and a polo shirt. His wife (I guessed by the ring) was sipping coffee.

"Um. Excuse me, sir," I interrupted them. "Can I ask you a question?"

He looked at me. "Yes, you may." He took his sunglasses off. His wife had long blond hair and was attractive in a suburban kind of way. Nails red. Perfect makeup. Body by Curves.

"This fine-looking woman sitting here at this table has just turned me down on a proposal to kiss her and the only way I can get my dignity back is if I either kiss you or your fine wife here."

The wife chimed in. "You can kiss him. I certainly don't want to."

Mandy Weaver's mouth was gaping wide open.

"Ma'am, may I?" She nodded.

"Sir, may I?" He nodded.

I stood up, took two steps over to him and planted a smooch right on his lips.

"Thank you, sir. My kisser was needing that!"

"Glad I could oblige. The next beer is on me." He looked at Mandy and smiled at her.

"Piper, you are one crazy girl. I've never seen anything like you."

"And, you probably never will. Come with me for a drive up this cool road I found?" I asked her swallowing the remnants of beer number three.

"Piper, you're scaring me. Plus, I think Kara might be coming to meet us."

"Call her and tell her you've canceled the plan and have to go over some inside moves with the new first-year pussy from Canada." I waved for the tab. I was getting a buzz but a sobery one.

Mandy picked up her phone and texted Kara. "I don't feel much like talking anyway."

"Good. There will be no talking while I drive you and Someday down this pretty road then. Capische?"

"What, are you suddenly Jewish?"

"No, I just like the language and don't get me all ver klempt looking out at the serene countryside. You'll make me long for home and then I'll really have to kiss you."

Mandy grabbed the tab as the waitress laid it on the table. "Well, if you are going to kidnap me then I should pay the price, now, shouldn't I?"

"I charge a lot more than this place does." I nodded my thanks. "Come on Someday." I re-clipped her leash and picked up the water bowl for her. I asked her for a few tricks: one-paw, two-paw then a good loud speak. She got three treats and we nearly cleared the restaurant of patrons because her barker was in full throttle. Good girl.

When we got to the truck, I opened the club cab and Someday put her front paws on the backseat and then I lifted her the rest of the way in. Her arthritis was hurting her, I could tell, so I had to help her up. Grabbing Mandy's laptop bag and backpack, I put them both in the back with mine. I silently stroked my notebook in a prayerful way and heard a distant clanging noise.

She got in the passenger side. "I only have an hour before I need to get back to my dorm. I have to study!"

"Don't worry, I'll get you to the church on time," I said.

"I do believe you have kidnapped me from responsibility. I'm half-drunk and there's a lame dog and a girl who's very full of herself driving me off campus and up a country road." Mandy looked for a CD as she said this.

"I told you 'no talking.'" I turned the ignition and turned to pat Someday on the head.

"What CD do you want to hear?"

"Anything by Patty Griffin. She's the best of the best."

She rummaged through my console of CDs and buzzed the window down. The wind blew in and messed up her hair. She looked up at me. "This one looks good. *A Thousand Kisses.* Sounds like something you would listen to to get your kisser up." She laughed and put it in.

"Getting your kisser up is a good thing. Luckily that man back there was willing. Looks like it will be the luckiest part of my day besides doing tricks with my dog."

"I'm glad you're on the team, Piper. We need some fresh blood. Plus, I think Coach Potter and Coach DuPont like you."

"How so?"

"Coach Potter is really cool and has a certain finesse at handling players. She's always looking out for her players. Saneha gets into it all the time but she likes her, too. Sometimes she just doesn't show it."

"Natalie Wingfield told me that Coach Potter is gay. True?"

"Yeah. But she hides it because of the parents, the school and the media. Three institutions she doesn't want jading her in any way."

"Wow. Copasetic. Now you've used jaded. You know your English, girl."

Mandy Weaver didn't say anything to that because the music started the Patty Griffin flotation like it always did when that girl sang. The prettiest lyrics and music I'd ever heard. Perfect, since the girl next to me was hot, and I had my dog in the back with her head stuck out the window.

Just off Route 250 was Route 20 north which wound its way toward Barboursville. The road started off with a stoplight, but within seconds my truck was wheeling through the syncopation of the vibration where tire met tar and gripped through tight curves and then slow ones. The bends in the road made my stomach stir and I pressed on the accelerator at the peak of each rise and then let go so the truck would fly. It was bliss, suddenly. Driving was bliss. Nothing keeping me at my apartment, nothing keeping me behind a computer, nothing keeping my mind imprisoned at night; just attention to the truck and the past we created in back, the present we held with the cows and the sodden grass God had laid down right out of the sky and the dark brown fences lining up the land with order, and the horses who looked when I tooted the horn and waved at them; the future, just ahead around the bend and pregnant in my mind's eye. What sign would be there? Would it be a deer crossing? Would it be a route number and an arrow to the left? Would it be a road sign that said Sacred Meadow? Would it be a Civil War marker of the ghosts of men and women who'd created their own past, present and future—the way I was creating mine, not on horseback or afoot, but in a truck with a girl, not a boy?

Turn here. An arrow. I did.

"Can I talk now?" Mandy asked turning the volume down.

I nodded. "Two minutes. Give me two minutes." I didn't know what that meant, but knew a road sign would tell me when to stop. We drove through a one-lane bridge where you had to honk the whole time through. Then I looked to my left and saw a large rock with a pointer at the top of it. Chiseled out just for me, I thought. This must be the place to stop. Just up around that bend.

It was a steep incline and then the road leveled out and then to the left there was a sign that said Turtle Crossing. I laughed and thought, slow down. I did so, then I pulled over into the gravel bend on the side of the road and showed Mandy Weaver something I had never seen before but the signs had gotten me there. A vista. A vista that was lined with fencing around the edges, a small creek that smelled like gravel and rock through my open window, a vista where oak trees framed a community of nature we humans had no right bothering. The leaves were rich and lusty and green and the sun dispatched tendrils of light and warmth over the veins of leaves, feeding them with a nourishment that would carve in and out of the fleshy insides through the stems to the bark through the many layers of wood down into the root and the movement down would be slow and the surge that pushed and pulled through the aged ground would do its own urge. Nature in Virginia. Perhaps Canada was level playing ground to this. My brain felt like a microcosm to this macrocosm. Could it be parallel?

Strange thinking. I reached to touch Someday's fur.

"It's beautiful," Mandy said. "Come on, let's get out and take Someday over there."

"Okay." It was all I could manage in my sudden cataleptic state. I put my hands to my head and smoothed my curls back. I heard from the large rock a clanging noise. A noise I thought Mandy might have heard but she did not. It scared me slightly but I dismissed it when I saw a goose and her goslings march across a small path to the pond that lay to the left of my view. There were seven of them altogether. They waddled and marched and I pointed so Mandy could see them.

"Oh, my, they're so cute." Mandy stopped to ponder them. I looked at her body in a lusty way. She was tender and quiet and sweet, not like some of the girls I'd dated before. She reminded me of one of my schoolteachers from back home who'd always paid extra close attention to me. Oh, God, here comes a crush . . .

The energy was all over me like an electric blanket gone short circuit and nipping its surges in the back of my neck, then in the palms of my hands, and then in my stomach, and down my legs. Mainly, though, in my stomach. She turned toward the sun and then put her sunglasses on. Clanging. I turned toward the rock and thought I saw a figure pop up from behind. Neon red and blue, it waved, then shot back down. When my head returned, Mandy had taken two steps closer to me.

"How'd you find this place?"

"Blind leading the blind, I guess. You know any good reasons not to kiss?" I swallowed from a can of warm beer and regarded her.

"How about I think we are in a wide open space and I'm not sure who lives in that farmhouse over there. It could be something out of some scary movie. I don't want to make the evening news."

"Hold my hand then, Mandy Weaver. I promise we won't make the evening news if you promise not to let go for the minutes it takes us to get to that vista over there." I pointed.

"Okay. But no kissing."

"No kissing. I promise."

She smiled. "I feel kind of weird holding your hand, especially after you just kissed some random guy in a restaurant. What if you carry some hetero disease I don't want to catch?" She fumbled in the grass and lost her footing.

I squeezed her hand and helped her balance. "I got you."

"Whoa. Sorry about that." Then she giggled.

"See. If you talk like that, it will get you nowhere. It'll make your steps unsteady and you'll fall over."

"What if I said, kiss me?" She was flirting back.

"Then I'll fall over and we'll be in a snarl on the ground and then I will make you a kissing sandwich you'll want to re-taste for days."

"What, 'cause it will put me in a daze?" Now she was a word-smith.

"But of course, I am here to daze you, Weaver. I like that name Weaver."

"Just don't call me Dream Weaver. I've had to put up with that my entire life."

"Oh, it's so hard," I said.

"What?"

"Your life. It's so hard putting up with that epithet. Are you okay? Do you need to sit down from the burden of it all?"

"I'm going to kick your ass in basketball practice tomorrow. You just wait."

"That's the problem with people like me Dream Weaver—"

"What's that?"

"I can't wait. So you can either kiss me now, or we can go on with this flirty behavior till I corner you on the baseline and kiss you in front of Coach Potter. Or you can wait till I kick your ass playing ping. Or you can wait till I write the greatest poem of all time about you and they publish it in the *Virginia Quarterly Review* for the whole literary world to see. I'm writing either a great love poem or a great book. Or you can wait till I'm thirty and have kissed every man in every restaurant from here to San Diego."

"If you kiss me in front of Coach Potter, she'll probably kick us both off the team and send us to that coach in Maryland so she can put us on the right programs to hetero-hood."

"Done. I will kiss you tomorrow and make you pregnant." I laughed and ran down the hill with Someday.

"Pregnant. Piper. How are you going to make me pregnant? By the way, what's the *Virginia Quarterly Review*?"

I ignored her and ran down the hill to the creek below, Someday galloping five feet behind me. I was laughing and Mandy was laughing and I didn't have a care in the world. When I got to the edge of the bend in the brook, my flip-flop slipped on the edge. I toppled four feet down and into the water. Someday slid down from behind and entered the water with me. Good girl. The water was not very deep and I lay there like the lady in the lake till Mandy approached and looked onto the crime scene.

"Grace? That's your new name, Grace?"

"Yes?"

"You okay?"

"No."

"What can I do?"

"Kiss the frog."

"Kiss the dog?" She couldn't hear me.

"Yes, kiss the dog, you spazoid. Get down here and help me up before the English get here and find that I've lost the key to the city and we'll be eating pine nuts till the French throw down the gauntlet."

Mandy slid down the hill, stepped into the water, and then held out her hand. I was tempted to pull her in but could tell by her squeamish look that that would be a bad idea.

"Piper you are weird. But, I like you. I'm not sure what a gauntlet is, but I do like you."

"Someday likes you for sure. But since I haven't kissed you, I'm not sure if I like you. We must flirt for at least seven more days."

"Why seven more days?"

"Did you hear that?"

"What?"

"That clanging noise?"

"No, what clanging noise?"

"Like someone is banging on hot iron clanging noise. Hold my hand, Mandy. The French must be coming to get the English. I feel as if the Battle of Orleans is ensuing. We must flee back to my apartment before the arrows fly."

"Piper, shut up." She laughed and put her hands on her knees.

"Come on. I need to get back and study. And you need to get ready for an ass-whipping at tomorrow's practice."

She grabbed my hand and the noise stopped. We walked back to my truck with Someday at our heels.

"We'll come back here sometime if you want, Dream Weaver. You can spin a tall tale for me in that scientific mind of yours. Calculate a word problem or two for me. Draw a map of your life on a napkin we get from a sandwich store. Thanks for holding my hand."

"You're welcome. And, yes, I can do that," she said. "It's nice here. I feel like I'm a million miles away from the pressure of school and basketball and Coach Potter."

"Does she pressure you?"

"No. Not too much." She looked away.

"I do know some cool spots in Richmond. My hometown. Maybe you could go there with me sometime?"

"Maybe."

"Maybe is not a good enough word. Come on, you've used some good ones. Maybe isn't clear enough. It's muddy and uncertain and . . ." I leaned closer to her, "Wobbly and just kind of plain and nothing and . . ."

"Shut up. I'll go with you to Richmond sometime."

"Shut up? How about clamp it. Shut it. Put a vise on it. Seal it—"

"Oh, God—"

"He's got nothing to do with it," I said.

She leaned closer. "Nothing to do with what?"

I stepped back. "He has nothing to do with anything."

She opened the truck door. Someday whined. Moving over in the grass, I accidentally brushed against Mandy. "I thought you prayed?" she asked.

"I do. I pray, but I also do battle."

"With what?"

"I feel like I've been battling the whole world my whole life. Like Joan of Arc, a bit misunderstood, perhaps. I'm just weird, Weaver. Don't worry about it."

"I think you're smart."

"Really?"

"Yeah. You're the first dumb freshman I've ever liked."

"Thanks for the paradox."

"Well, I'm not sure what that means. But glad I could help."

"That's the spirit! Keep it up Weaver. Want another beer?"

We drove back to BRU feeling buzzy and silly. Weaver relaxed some more and Someday held her head out the window. For a few brief moments in the fall of my first semester in college, I did not feel homesick for Canada. This was good.

Two days later, I got a copy of *The Awakening* by Kate Chopin in the mail from Vera. Tattered and worn, it smelled like an old classic with yellowed pages and a font that was worn out and dog-eared pages marking either importance or a good place to stop.

Chapter 5

My bed was dank—saturated with my own urine. I had slept in it. Awakening from what was an induced coma, I unsealed my salty eyes and looked out the barred window. A long row of Japanese maple trees hovered near the sidewalk and the road sharing the common boundary of Noon Bridge where people in white coats underneath winter jackets milled as the winter wind whipped up a whirl that made small eddies of leaves. Embarrassed. I was embarrassed by my childlike behavior: wetting the bed. Then I remembered the voice that told me do so.

I looked to the vent. No snake. The room was white and my door was open to the hallway where I saw several patients walking by and a nurse's attendant waving a clipboard to a doctor that passed by. The room bent itself to the side. There was an ashen feel, a dreariness in the walls, almost macabre. There was numbness in my hands and I pulled them from under the covers. Gazing at my palms, I saw an oily sweat above the head line, the heart line, and the head line. Palmistry: I'd studied it a bit along with Tarot cards. Andrea was an aficionado.

When I looked at my hospital wristband, it said, Cullen Cliff— my mother's name. This wasn't right and I knew it. I closed my eyes to see if it would change to mine. It did not. I closed them again, harder this time. Still, it said my mother's name. My stomach dropped, my nerves pushed out from my skin, surfacing like a million periscopes. For God's sake, just look away.

When I did, I noticed I was not alone in my room. There was another bed. Had I been moved? What day was it? Where was I? I suddenly thought of Someday and saw her face when I closed my eyes. It comforted me in the solitary confinement of my mind. I put my hands to my face where she'd licked me a million times—I could almost feel her cold wet nose. Good girl. Good Someday. Here she was comforting me in the spaces in between us. *That's the spirit.*

There was an older woman in the bed next to me who was lying on her side facing me. She had salt-and-pepper hair and her wrinkles looked like dark, dirty crevices. She looked filmy, like a black and white shadow, real and unreal at the same time. I couldn't figure out the difference. Next to the bed was her walker. There was a glass box on the table behind her. Her shoulder blocked what was in it but I already could feel it was there. The snake meant to bite me. It obviously had slithered through the vent during my sleep, or perhaps she brought it here on her own. The snake I was meant to eat and shit out to conjugate my own fear and to purge the evil from the world of paralysis, pedophiles and torturers in the physical and metaphysical worlds. What a job this was going to be! I fell back on the bed and looked to the vent then back through the barred window. *Someone help! Please, I need some help. I can't do this on my own. I need some serious help.* My gaze turned back to her.

When she opened her eyes, I asked who she was because her face changed to black and white and her hair began to stand up all around her head. Chills ran concurrent with the breathiness that consumed my chest and I peed a bit in my pants. Squeezing my legs together, I looked quickly into the mirror at myself at the end of the room above the bureau just below the vent. My hair stood up behind my head just like hers, like electricity had shot up through the follicles on my cranium and had given the back of my head little hair erections all over. I was a mash of freckles and curly hair and eyes sunken and drawn from weeks of sleepless nights, weeks of figuring out the connective tissue of the world and how it all related to Einstein's theory of relativity and how Jesus Christ had marched with the bishops of the Roman Catholic church all the way to Texas where they chopped off his head and threw it in the Gulf of Mexico. I drew a complete map of the travels and tried to convince the Episcopal priest I met on one of my drives how important that was and that we needed to send some anthropologists there to find his decapitated head. Do not, I repeated on many occasions, ask the mappers of the roads of Charlottesville. Christ's head was deep in the Gulf near Corpus Christi . . . duh, the writing was already on the map. They were going to need plenty of rodeo girls to show them the way down there because women were part of the millionth circle of light and knew the way better than men. Plus they looked really cute all dressed up riding the hell out of those horses. Why everyone looked at me funny when I tried to explain my thoughts and theories was beyond me. It made complete and utter sense. I knew because I was sent to let the world know that there had been some mistakes and that there was a plan to help get it all fixed up. Namely, my womanifesto.

"My name is Rose," she said. Her voice was male and deep and throaty and slow. She had a man's voice.

I asked, "Can I use your walker to get to the end of the bed?"

"Sure you can."

"I just need some help to the end of the bed, and I think I'll be all right."

I stood up. My jeans were soaked all the way across my hips, and I needed to get to the end of the bed to get to my bag. I grabbed the walker and shook the whole way to the end where I sat down and looked into the mirror again. My hair was down. Good. I smoothed it back with my hands and tried to make small talk with Rose who sounded like a man.

"Why are you here?" I asked, looking back at her.

She turned in her bed a bit and put her arm over her head. Then she morphed completely before my eyes. Holy shit! From a woman to a man in black and white right before my eyes. Her dark eyes became large almonds and her hair darker and shorter and her eyebrows became longer and her whole face pinched like a prune. "I am here because my legs hurt and I'm a little confused." Deep and guttural it came.

Looking away, I was suddenly frozen. I looked for my shoes and hoped that the spiders would not return. I thought about the glass case behind Rose and tried not to think about it. I hummed a slow tune making it up as I went along. I pulled my pants off and returned to a thought. "I'm a little confused, too. Thanks for letting me use your walker."

I reached quickly into my bag hoping no snakes would slither out. The one in the glass case was the special one, I knew. But, perhaps she had friends that were following me. What was worse snakes or spiders? I did not know. They both were bad evils and I wasn't happy that my worst nightmares were getting picked on.

Rose yawned and scratched the underside of her belly. "You were a bit confused last night in your sleep. You kept talking about spirits and bridges and delivering mail. Weird combination. Do you deliver mail?"

"No, Jenny does," I said, pressing my hands on my head to make sure my hair was down. Jenny had carried mail in Virginia and back home in Banff. One summer over six years ago, she had taken me and Someday on a million rides in her postal truck. How she never hit a mailbox going as fast as she went always amazed me.

Just as I was buttoning a fresh pair of jeans, Paige came into the room and smiled at me. Her khaki pants were loose around her waist and her blue button-down shirt had her hospital ID hanging on the pocket. She had a clip in her hair and her mole maintained perfect stillness this time.

"Sorry about the bed," I said. Smoothing my hair back, I pulled a cap over my head so my hair would stay down. Rubbing my palms on my thighs, I looked back at Rose and could not make out the glass case.

"You've got some people here who want to see you. Jenny and Vera. They've come a long way from Canada, I hear, and want to see you. You've been sleeping off and on for over thirty-six hours. They're really itching to talk to you."

Then it came. The fog inside my head rolled in and my eyes burned and the fear welled up like electric biting filaments coming out through my head and skin.

"Can I smoke first?" I asked.

"You're an athlete!" She put her hands on her waist.

I smiled at her and looked behind me. "Athletes are best known for their covert activities. Smoking and drinking are two of mine—sometimes flirting."

She smiled. "Well, you've already flirted with me and if your coach knows you're smoking, she may have apoplexy."

"Who's that?"

"Your basketball coach. Now—"

I stood up. "Who is this lady in the bed next to me?" My hands shook and I shoved them in my pocket.

"I told you, I'm Rose," she said like Linda Blair incarnate.

"Jenny and Vera are in the visitors waiting room." Paige stripped the sheets to my bed. "Why don't you hold off on the cigarette till you have talked to them. You can all eat breakfast together downstairs. Sound good?"

"Who's Jenny, Jenny, Jenny?" I asked and then quickly pulled my hands out and placed them both over my mouth. I did not want to begin yelling her name. Confusion laid its thick tarry hand on me.

"You don't know who Jenny is?" Paige looked at me weird, and cocked her head to the side. Bad question. Okay, needed to rethink that one.

"Jenny and Vera raised you in Canada—remember?"

"I was raised in Richmond, Virginia."

"Oh, you were. Well, word has it, you were raised in Canada."

"Victor lives in Richmond," I said. "Jenny . . . Rose . . . Rose . . ."
I turned my head to look around the room and got dizzy.

"Who's Victor?"

"My grandfather, the devil incarnate. Or maybe Rose is?"

"Hey, I heard that," came her normal voice.

"Sorry, Rose."

"That's okay. Remember, you used my walker."

"I've got my palm juice all over it."

Lurking outside of my room was Uno girl and the dark criminal
I'd first encountered in the foyer who knows how many hours earlier.
He twiddled his hair and stood about four inches from Uno girl's
toes. Smoking was a good thing. Clear the air. Clear the bad juice. I
scratched the insides of my palms then looked down at them. Spirals.
Large spirals moving molecularly clockwise in my hands.

Then time stopped.

Reaching out to touch the arc in my right palm, I remembered
suddenly why Ulysses had traveled away from the Charybdis and
closer to the Scylla. If he went closer to the snaky rocks, then he'd
lose six of his men. If he went closer to the Charybdis, they all died—
all of them, swallowed up in the swirl of the sea.

"Will you hold my hand?" I looked at Paige.

"Sure, come on. Let me walk you down to see your people, okay?
Rose, I'll be right back."

Turning from my room to the foyer of the ward, I saw couches
of people sitting everywhere. The dark criminal quickly sat down
with Uno girl and when I caught his eye, I mouthed, *Stay away from
her.* He laughed and looked through me like a knife was cutting my
throat or something. I then mouthed *Mother fucker.* But it came out
full vocal.

Everyone in the waiting room looked at me. I then said that it
was okay. "No spiders today, just a mother fucking pedophile!" Then
I glared at him.

"Watch your mouth, girl! Lord!"

"Paige, we need to get rid of all the perverts and rapists and mur-
derers and pedophiles. Everywhere." I tried to whisper but said *every-*

where three times before I could shut up my adult-onset Tourette's.

"Well, I agree with that." She held my hand and led me down a corridor past six or seven wheelchairs and the exhausted people half-splayed out in them.

I turned into the waiting room and found Vera and Jenny sitting on a couch. Vera had her nose in a book and Jenny was on her cell phone. Vera had on jeans and a white T-shirt with a sweater vest. Her hair was cut short and straight and it was grayer than when I'd last seen her. Jenny had on cargo pants and a blue sweatshirt that said *Irish*. She'd gotten word, I guessed, that blue was the better color to wear around me. At once, they looked up to me and both got up and walked toward me, slightly hesitant.

"Hey, guys," I managed.

"Piper, you look like you haven't slept in the three months since I've seen you. Here give me a hug." Vera was a good six inches shorter than me and her head came right under my chin. She was round in the middle and her hands on my back and shoulder felt nice. "Did you read *The Awakening* by Chopin?" she asked as she released me.

Her lips and tongue changed shapes but I looked away. Paige put her hand on my shoulder, understanding, perhaps my fear and apprehension.

"I've missed you, too—and Someday, too!" We were in the waiting room outside the hallway where William James had his face inlaid in the tile—the hallway with the pretty oil paintings. "Did you see Mom and the pervert in there? I think this place is creepier than what's outside."

Jenny grabbed me quickly and said into my ear, "Piper, we're here for you honey. It's going to be okay. It's all okay. We brought you some stuff from Canada. You want to see?"

"Sure." I moved in Jenny's direction and then looked back at Paige.

"Go ahead, girl. There aren't any snakes over there. I can promise you that one."

"Tell him to leave the girl alone, Paige." I looked at her.

"Who?"

"That criminal sitting next to Uno girl."

"You mean Dickey, the big black guy with dreads, and Sally, the cute girl with long red hair?"

"Yes. Dickey and Sally. DS. Devil Snake. No, Dickey had six letters."

"Piper what in the hell are you talking about?" Jenny looked at Vera then at me.

"That Dickey guy in there is no good." I was perfunctory, telling what was being told to me. Then I looked out the window at Noon Bridge that crossed over the Rivanna River. "He hurts little girls. He's a licentious, rude, depraved scallywag—"

Vera laughed. "Have you been reading Mark Twain?"

"Dorothy Parker," I responded, then said, "Balderdash . . ." I giggled.

"Poppycock!" Vera laughed. "Good, she's more your speed." Then she pushed her reading glasses up on her nose and smiled at me.

Paige asked if we were through with the verbal word find and then told all of us to sit. We did.

She pulled out some papers and handed them to Vera and Jenny then began to talk like I wasn't in the room.

"Piper came in two days ago with her friend, Mandy Weaver, after quite the incident at John Paul Jones Arena. After a bit of a struggle, we got her to sign herself in and what we've noted here is that she is having psychotic bouts of grandiosity interspersed with some levels of reason. So, it's hard to tell when Piper is here with us or when she isn't."

"Paige, I'm right here," I said. "Jenny do you see me? Vera do you see me? This is all a sham. Vera, you have to listen to me. I've got something to tell you. You and Jenny will understand—"

They both nodded and looked at Paige. I was frustrated suddenly and looked out the window at the tree that was waving in the wind. It was a birch tree, I thought, but couldn't really tell. Branches, like arms, leaves like palms waving in the Virginia breeze. Waving at the divinity in me. I raised my hand and waved back.

"What are you waving at?" Vera asked.

"The tree. See, the one out there. Its branches are waving?"

Everyone looked to see if it was real. Of course it was.

"When a tree waves at you, you need to wave back," I said. "Jenny, you're tired of delivering mail, aren't you?"

"Yes, I am. Come sit over here next to me, Piper."

Paige continued. I sat next to Jenny and put my arm around her waist then rested my head on her shoulder. She put her arm around me and Vera sipped on some coffee. This was safe. Joan wasn't here yet with that white horse, but these two were safe right now. No snakes. Good. Just the licentious, lewd, bastard.

"Jenny? Do you see a worm back here in the back of my head?"

"No, honey, there isn't anything there." She stroked my head and I looked at Vera who caught my gaze. Her eyes turned to crosses and I closed my eyes.

"Dr. Spectrus has determined that Piper is experiencing symptoms of Bipolar Disorder. This is indicated by some of the things that Mandy left here with us and also by Teeter Mulligan who should be here any minute. Mandy left us with Piper's backpack, her journals, her rocks, her notebooks, her laptop. She also said that Piper has been visiting random hospitals in the area and asking handicapped patients if they needed help. She was kicked out of two hospitals, Mandy told us, and barely escaped being arrested after she struggled trying to get two patients out of their wheelchairs and into her car. They were elderly and Piper just took them from the hospital like she worked there."

"I was just trying to get them to see Christopher Reeve. Jenny, can you get Oprah or someone to get ahold of him? He's the only one who can make the snake thing happen."

Vera shifted in her seat. "Jenny do you know Christopher Reeve's phone number?"

Good Vera. *That's the spirit*, I thought.

"Christopher Reeve is dead," Jenny said flatly. "Piper, he died some time ago. Even his wife is gone. What's up with this snake thing? Hmm? I know you don't like snakes." She popped the top of my baseball cap and I pulled the brim back down.

"Nothing," I returned. Everyone thought Christopher Reeve was dead. Just his body, people. Just his body. Does it all have to be this elusive?

Suddenly, my home girl, Teeter Mulligan, came in through the door like she'd been thrown in on a tilt-a-whirl. She had on a baseball cap sideways like she and her homies did. Her wide gold grin was a surprise and I tried not looking at her eyes.

"Hey, Pipe. How you feeling? Are you still gay after all this or has there been a new age of enlightenment?" She came in with a paper bag and some flowers.

"Good Teeter, how are you feeling?"

"Well, you scared the hell out of us the other night with all your crazy ass talk at the tournament but other than that, I'm all right. Here." She reached in the bag. "I brought you some Slim Jims and some blond Oreos and your Tarot cards. I'm cool with the Slim Jims and the Oreos, but I'm not sure you need these Tarot cards with the way you've been talking." Teeter looked at Jenny and Vera. "When she pulls the ones with swords, she scares all of us. Theonia and Natalie are still taking the back way to their computer classes after what you said might happen to them."

Jenny grabbed them. "I'll take them. Andrea, my partner, got her into these years ago. Let's stick to some simple playing cards while you're here." Jenny shoved them in her pocket.

"Good to see you all again. Think the last time I saw you two was at the NCAA tournament last year in March, right? That was Piper's first trip here after signing on, right?" Teeter opened one of my Slim Jims and tore into it. She handed Vera one but she shook her head.

"Good to see you, Teeter," Vera said. "How's your mom's kidney dialysis going?"

"Good. She's doing a treatment every week. My dad said she'd live to be a hundred and die in her sleep. She just spins around in her wheelchair and smacks him on the head and tells him to make the coffee."

The bridge had bicyclers going across it, and Teeter's voice sounded strange, like she was talking in the eye of a vortex and in slow motion. Parents. I'd never heard of parents. Teeter's parents. She never talked of them. Clang. Clang. Clang. I held my breastplate and shut my eyes. *God just let me die.* I wanted to die. *Just let me die.* Yes. Let the umbrella of black envelop me. Anything, even death, was better than this. Where were the saints? Where were the Kennedys? Where was Robin Williams, for crying out loud?

"Where's Mandy?" I asked. No one paid attention to me. "Can Someday come and see me? Is Mandy with Coach Potter?"

"So, what can we do to help our girl here?" Teeter sat down.

"We can get your mom out of that wheelchair, Teeter," I said.

"You need to stop talking about saving people's asses in wheelchairs. That's something that the medical profession is in charge of, you gay bird, not you. Why the wheelchairs, Pipe? I don't get it. I understand the part about the perverts and all and some of your diagrams in your womanifesto . . . I just don't get the wheelchair part. S'up wif dat?" She looked at me cockeyed and I laughed.

"Teeter, you want to get a Coke with me?" Jenny asked.

Teeter popped up. "Sure. Need something to down these Jims with anyway . . ." They both walked out.

Paige exhaled deeply and then continued. "Well, we need some information filled out from you all—a family history to be specific. We also need to do a session with Dr. Spectrus . . ."

Then like out of a movie, Dr. Spectrus walked in. "Well, speak of the devil—" Paige winked at me.

"Rose is . . ." I trailed off.

He looked a bit like Ryan O'Neal. Dr. Spectrus had on a wrinkled white button-down shirt and glasses that made him look like Mr. Magoo. They were worse than Coke-bottle lenses. His eyelids must catch fire when he's in the sun, I thought. When he walked into the room, Vera stood up and everyone exchanged pleasantries. He asked me how I was and when his lips turned into worms, I just looked away and said, "Okay."

"Good. We've gotten you on some medication, Piper. But I hear from your roommate and your girlfriend that you've had quite the month on campus . . . especially the other night. How you didn't get arrested more than once is incredible."

"Am I in jail now?" I asked.

Paige whispered, "Just your mind, honey. Just your mind."

Vera went pale. "You got arrested?"

I whispered to her. "Vera, I've written a womanifesto. It's real. A real one."

She shrugged her shoulders a bit and whispered back, "Really?"

Jenny walked back in with Teeter. They both had drinks in their hands. Teeter was slurping on the edge of hers. "Who got arrested?" Jenny demanded.

"I did," I said. "With her." I pointed to Teeter.

"Now hold on, Piper. You got arrested. I just got a ticket for being disorderly."

"Will someone please tell me what's wrong with Piper?" Jenny sounded pissed.

Paige dropped her clipboard. "She's had a series of psychotic events . . ."

"Let me talk about that," Dr. Spectrus interrupted.

"Where were you arrested, Piper?" Vera asked me.

"On campus by the police . . . I was drunk and having a fight with Mandy."

"I told you I thought you were in too much with that Mandy girl." Vera flashed her eyes at Jenny.

Teeter pulled at her wig and sat down next to me. "We were outside of a campus pub and seems like my roomie here gets a little jealous over other women messing with her girl. Margaritas just added insult to insult. Piper can cuss like a sailor. The police didn't see any humor in that, now did they?" She looked at me and her eyes got big and round.

Jenny tried to keep the peace. "Okay, everyone just take a slide back to the left."

I got up and high-fived her. "That's the spirit, Jenny." I turned to Vera. "It's about two mountain girls, you see, and then a dog . . . and breaking ground to build a foundation for gay youth who need a retreat." I stared at Vera. She didn't say anything. "It's good, Vera. I did what you said and wrote all my ideas down. It's a great womanifesto. It has the Pope and Virginia Woolf, they get married. Then it has Peter Pan who finally gets some real wings and embraces the fact that he's gay. And Mary Poppins marries Helen Hunt in a civil union in Utah. How does it sound? Oh, and there are bishops everywhere and lots of bells and—" I stopped. Vera got up and started to cry.

"Did I make you read too many books?" Vera asked and blew her nose in a tissue Paige handed her.

"I must say," Teeter began, "she does know a little bit about a lot of things. It's hard to tell sometimes if what she sayin' is real or made up. She's got one large noodle in there." She tapped her head and looked at Jenny.

Jenny looked at Teeter. Teeter shrugged. "Well," Jenny said. "I always thought Mary Poppins had it in her. Who wouldn't want to marry Helen Hunt?"

"Did I fuck up?" I asked Jenny.

"No, honey, you didn't fuck up. You're just really tired."

Teeter looked at me. "Pipe, if you want to write about that stuff, you go right ahead. I'll read it."

"Mandy thinks it's all nutty. The things I write and say." I peered out the window.

Teeter got up and came over and hugged me. "Don't you worry now. Rest your head. It's in your spirit what you want to say, Piper. That's all. And, my momma says that what's in your spirit isn't something you own. It's something God gave you. You go on and write your thoughts down. I'll read it. I just don't understand the part about the paralyzed people. Maybe you can help me with that one?"

Dr. Spectrus, who'd been taking copious notes and keeping his head down, got up. "Maybe we should meet again in the morning. It looks like Piper could use some down time. I think this meeting has gotten her upset."

"You're upset, Dr. Speculum, not me," I said without looking at him. Why Teeter laughed at this, I did not know.

Dr. Spectrus shuffled his feet and crossed his arms in front of him, holy-like. "The thing we need here is a dose of medication to get you stabilized, Piper, and some rest. I asked Mandy how much alcohol you've been drinking. She said at least six drinks a night. Is that true?"

"No. More like ten or twelve. Did she mention the cocaine?"

"No," he said.

"Well, you should try it. It makes you the most interesting person in the room and you can stay up for three days straight or gay and it makes for torrid make-out sessions and conversation about everything from why the Contras got out of Honduras to how the politicians in America sold out to the Saudis more than twenty years ago and how our own weapons that we make here kill our own soldiers over there. Push your glasses up, Dr. Spectrus, and read the writing in my notebooks. You'll see why the world is so messed up."

"Mandy also told me that you failed English this semester. Is that true?" He pulled up his belt and stared down at me.

Right in front of Vera and Jenny, it stung. Failing my best subject made me incredulous all over again. "It was the teacher. He didn't understand my angles, and my thesis on E.M. Forster's *A Room with a View* was right on. It was him who was fucked up. Not me."

Dr. Spectrus pushed his glasses up. "In your transcript of grades here, it says that you barely passed history, you dropped ethics, and you got a C in both psychology and math. You did earn a B in Yoga?" he questioned me on the last one.

"I'm the best at downward facing dog." I stood up and stretched. "Where's Someday, anyway? Teeter, can you bring her here?"

Teeter's shoulders went down. "You been thinking about Someday?"

"Her and heaven, mostly. Heaven's only twenty-six miles away. Right, Teeter?"

Now, Jenny started to cry. Shit. That was hard to do.

Dr. Spectrus smoothed out his shirt and inhaled deeply. "I think we should meet again tomorrow when the medication has had another full twenty-four hours to integrate into her system."

Vera came up to me. "Piper . . . have you been thinking about your folks and heaven? It's okay if you have. I know you miss them, honey. Maybe going to Richmond to see your grandfather was too much, huh?"

"Is Mandy coming with Someday?" I asked.

Jenny went through the door with her hand cupped over her mouth. Teeter came up from behind me. "I don't know. We'll see what we can do."

My chest hurt and I could barely breathe when I saw them all walk down the corridor over the top of William James' mosaic tile and through the door with the big Exit sign overhead. All I longed for now was to have my dog with me and for Mandy to come. I tried to mouth their names in the air. I could form Mandy's name silently, but when I began to say my dog's name, I grabbed my neck and started to choke.

"Come on, Piper. It's been a long couple of hours."

Paige's third eye was barely visible and I concurred. Looking through the window again, I saw my family and Teeter walk slowly to freedom through the parking lot without me. Dr. Speculum examined me from afar and I gave him the finger. His eyes crossed and I squeezed Paige's hand.

Just past the janitor's dirty linen cart I slowly walked, re-grabbing Paige's hand for security purposes. She got me a bottle of water from the nurses' station behind the bulletproof glass and gave me a blue pen and a pad of paper I'd asked her for. Most of the nurses had their noses to some chart or were on the phone talking about medication and dosage amounts. Paige escorted me into the room next to the station, a rec room with chairs and tables and sofas and old, outdated games and tray tables. The people on TV were throwing snakes at each other. I knew this was not real but couldn't help but stare at it anyway. My elbows started to shake almost uncontrollably. The room had a large window that gave view to the parking lot on the east side of the hospital where cars were lined up like little tin soldiers waiting to roll home on command.

Paige said, "The medication may make you shake a little."

"Why is everyone in a wheelchair?" I hugged my shoulders to stop my arms from shaking.

Paige looked around. "Honey, no one is in a wheelchair in here. Is that what you see? Hmmm. People in wheelchairs?"

"No." I lied. But, they were everywhere—all looking at me for the answer with vacant eyes and still bodies. I needed to write this down, perhaps make a list of names.

Sally, the Uno girl, laughed a little when she heard Paige and me talking. She was hunched over the cards and rubbing her thighs like she was going to start a fire. Then she suddenly got up and came over to me. Her legs wobbled and she looked like she might fall over.

"You want to play cards?" she asked. "Hey, we can sit here." She pointed. Her hands were shaking violently when she rubbed the hair from her eyes. Paige went back toward the sixteen people now rolling in wheelchairs down the corridor behind the bulletproof glass. Everyone was gone. Vera and Jenny and Teeter were gone. My eyes scanned the room. What event would take place now? *If I can't have Teeter and Someday and my parents*, I whispered, *perhaps a few saints or apostles. Anyone, anyone, anyone* . . . I prayed in my head and closed the fog out in my head. When people left, everything crumbled. I just didn't know it was the trigger.

"Okay. Where's that guy?"

"What guy?"

"The guy who's been bugging you . . . black guy with dreds . . . the criminal," I said.

"Oh, you mean, Dickey. He's okay."

"Don't let him near you. He's a criminal, criminal, criminal." I sat down across the table from her. Her eyes did not turn to crosses. Thank God.

"Okay, I heard criminal the first time. Do you remember how to play?" She held the cards and shuffled them.

"No."

It took her about fifteen minutes to describe how to play what I kept thinking was a simple game. Then I got distracted by the sudden appearance of all of the Hollywood movie stars and politicians that entered the room. Marilyn Monroe, white blond and gay came in as a nurse holding a chart and winking at me. She wasn't Joan of Arc but she looked good anyhow. Sally kept explaining and I just wanted her to shut up. I put my hands on my head and cupped my eyes. Surreal facing real, or was it the opposite? The inside of my head felt like the Fall of the House of Usher—a gray crumbling cryptic mass all melting together, sulphuric, misty red, macabre. Then there he was—Bobby Kennedy, plain as day, pushing his brother in a wheelchair. Houdini came in with his arms hugging himself but he was strapped to nothing. Black-and-white film. It was all black-and-white film. Then after that Nelson Mandela appeared in drag with Barbra Streisand. He pushed her in a wheelchair, too. I had to stare at everything and the litany of these people who were arriving interrupted my game with Sally Uno. A man who looked like David Letterman in disguise asked me if I wanted to read his poem. I kindly told him no thank you maybe later. Then there was Mom. She was still on my wristband—now here with me, the undead. Sally Uno kept on describing how to play the game and how the cards matched up. I didn't care suddenly as I watched my mom talk to Nelson Mandela and hold Barbra Streisand's hand. She then walked by Bobby Kennedy and smoothed his hair back and then put the back of her hand on John's face. They smiled.

"Mom," I called. "Can you get the number for Christopher Reeve? Maybe Robin Williams has it? Can you call him? Why is this so hard?"

Uno girl put the cards into play. "You ready? Is your mom here? Do you need to talk to her first?"

"No, she knows the plan. It's just taking forever to get there and it's starting to piss me off."

"PISSED OFF!" Uno girl barked out. Everyone looked at her. We both looked at each other and laughed. "PISSED OFF. Now pick a card before it's FUCK OFF," she barked at me.

"What do you have? Why are you here?" I asked. "Can you help me?"

"FUCK off! The cards talk to me. Now let's play. Hurry before they make us stop."

The first card I picked had a big O on it and then I became confused. Full circle? Did I write that one down? Big O. Full circle. Paige came to me and handed us both pills to take along with a cup of water that shook so violently in Sally Uno's hand she could barely get any in her mouth. A male nurse from behind the counter came over and sat on the couch near us and brought a box of pens and pencils and crayons and sheets of paper. He laid them all on the table next to us and some of the celebrities came over to have a coloring party. He said that if they all just stood around time would stand still and nothing would happen. A tall guy named Buster who looked like a Vietnam throwback told him about the bombs exploding over in China.

I picked up a second card. The image was red and bloody and its guts oozed from the card. Across the top was a stringy mass, across the bottom was an ancient language where the T looked like the cross and it talking to me in a strange burbling call I could not make out. Cutting my eyes to Sally, I laid it down on a stack.

"Is that right?" I pushed out of my lips. I looked down at my shoelaces. No spiders. But a snake was about to come in the room. The hair on my neck stood up. Where was Rose?

"YESSSSSSS!!! That's right! About time. YOU ARE SLOW!" She laughed and so did I, but I was not comfortable.

After a moment of silence, I methodically flipped another card to come into my view. There it was. A red snake. I thought it would arrive in my food or in my orange juice or in the floating smoke of one of my cigarettes. But, nevertheless, there it was. Its tongue was splayed out and it became larger than the card I held. I spat at it then licked the card to get the demons out. The people in this room were too precious for this one. I had to get the demon out.

"YOU are SICK!" Sally Uno barked at me in laughing disgust, then licked one of her own. We sat there, flipping cards and licking them till Paige came around the corner and told us we needed to color instead. She put some paper and drawing implements on the table, namely crayons, and told us to lower our voices.

I sidled beside Nelson Mandela who smelled like patchouli oil and I took a large piece of paper and began to draw the sweetest dog in the world: Someday.

I rocked as I drew her. Her blue head had floppy ears and then I put the mascot vest around her body and swathed out a funky paw. When I was done, I kissed the drawing and put her name underneath it. Then I started a new picture of Mom and Dad and my brother Jack. When I began to moan, Sally Uno came over and sat next to me and asked me what was WRONG?

"My family died," I said.

"That SUCKS! What happened?"

"Car crash. Car crashes SUCK! My drunken driving grandfather is a FUCK!" I yelled.

Nelson Mandela put his hand over mine. "A lot of shit in this world sucks, my dear. Losing loved ones is one of them. Jail is another."

Barbra Streisand leaned over me and said, "Anxiety sucks, too."

"So does a short life." John Kennedy looked at me and winked. "My cat, Lucy, died when she was young." I winked back a thank you. "Now that I think about it, convertibles suck, too." Everyone laughed.

"Nine-to-five jobs suck," Marilyn Monroe said. "I hated my nine-to-five job. Too many pills suck, too." Her hand went to her stomach.

"Maybe we should all smoke. I need to breathe," said David Letterman. He had on pin-striped pants and a white T-shirt with yellow-stained armpits.

Everyone agreed and we marched like ants into the smoking lounge. It was an anteroom to the rec room where the smell of stale smoke permeated the air and the two couches were old black leather ones from the 1950s. The coffee table had *People* magazine, the *New York Times* and *Highlights*. An odd mix, I thought. There was a Bible on the end table that thankfully was not speaking to me as the magazine had a few days earlier. The lamp shades on both end tables had fringe hanging down from them. They looked hairy. A small chill came over me.

One of the male attendants pulled out a box of cigarettes and we all grabbed one. There was a lighter built into the wall and you had to put your face up to it and insert the cigarette into the small cylinder, push a button, and it flamed up to light the end. My eyes got big as I could not stop staring at the flame. I wiped my hands on my pants and drew in a big furl of smoke.

When I turned to look at the people around the coffee table in this sitting room, something was different. Their faces had changed and were in color again. Rose was there and she stared at me. She was all right, I thought. But who were these people? Marilyn Monroe was older and heavier. Her hair was stringy and did not puff out like before. Bobby and John were older, too. John walked on his own and Bobby sat away from him next to Nelson Mandela who was really Dickey Dred. Everyone else was different, too. Different people.

Picking up a magazine on the coffee table and inhaling deeply from my cigarette, I overheard one of them say, "When she conjugates the snake, she'll be back to normal. She's gonna have to shit that bastard out."

I looked up to see a black-and-white Robin Williams looking at me. His eyes went to heaven. "Chris told me that if you shit out the snake, Piper, you will have cast out the demon. It's not going to be easy. Look for the palms. They will help you. Look for the palms by your bed."

I cried inside, deep and hard. Robin Williams. Holy cow. Palms?

"Can Chris help?" I asked. "I just need to know if he can help? There are so many paralyzed people. I know he can help. I've been watching him since I was a kid on the big screen. I know he's got it in him. Can you ask him?"

"He knows, Piper. He's sending in your angels. They come in many forms, so pay attention, okay?"

"Okay."

Then I asked, "Is he okay?"

"Who?" Robin Williams began to disappear into the couch.

"Christopher Reeve."

"You mean Superman?" He went into the couch.

I took a long drag from my cigarette and looked nervously around to see if anyone else had noticed my conversation with Robin FUCK-ING Williams. No one seemed jarred by it.

"After I bombed them Nammy bitches at the Tet Offensive, well . . ." Buster was speaking up for the first time in smoke group. "Well, I just thought if I can get back home after this shit and get a piece of land and a wife and then drink Jack Daniels for the rest of my life, well then, HELL, that would be all right."

"HELL!" Sally yelled.

"HELL!" everyone yelled.

Buster laughed. "And then I could get me some money from the government and then I could have an apple orchard where me and my Asian-ass wife would live up in the mountains of West Virginia, and then I could practice shooting my guns at cans instead of people and that would be better. Shoot the can. Kick the can. Hide and go seek."

"Hide and go seek." Dickey, the criminal, looked at me. "That's a fun game. Like Truth or Dare. Anyone ever play Truth or Dare."

"Madonna has." The old David Letterman exhaled his smoke.

"Truth or Dare—anyone?"

"DARE!" Sally Uno waved in the air.

"I like a good dare." Harry Houdini had his arms wrapped around his waist and it was the first time he'd spoken. Tricky. Very tricky, I thought. He kept his arms around himself every time he took a drag from his cigarette. His eyes were sunken and he was gaunt.

Dickey whispered in Harry's ear and they both laughed. Suddenly and out of nowhere, Harry started to cry.

"Don't cry, Harry," I said.

"My name's not Harry. I told you that before. It's Gerald. Stop calling me Harry." He got up snuffed out his cigarette and put his arms back around his body.

"I dare you to sit next to me," Dickey told Sally Uno.

"That's a STUPID dare," she responded.

"Then sit on my lap," he said.

"FUCK you!" I barked and then the male attendant came in and stopped our shenanigans.

Dickey walked by me and grabbed my hand, "Truth or Dare to be continued later." I pulled my hand away and longed for Paige to see what was going on and then before I knew it Hilary Swank was walking into the room. Black and white, again.

"Got a phone call from my sister the other day," she said, sitting down and taking a long drag. Her legs were shaking and she crossed them, then smoothed out her pants and resumed. "California is so ahead of us in so many things that they've gotten behind us." She laughed nervously. "L.A. and Hollywood are becoming so much less fashionable than they used to be. She says that many people are getting the hell out because they can't stand the egos and narcissism of the entire state. It's like California is kissing her own ass and it feels so good, she can't stop paying attention to herself." She took a long drag and then her paranoia set in. "Know what I mean? Know what I mean? Know what I mean?"

Buster dropped his bomb. "Mean. Yes. I know what mean is."

Nelson Mandela got up and stretched. "I think California is nirvana."

"Shut up, Buddha, and have a seat," Robert Kennedy barked and then readjusted the leveling on John's chair. "California is fine but it's no nirvana."

"Neither is Texas," John laughed.

"The head of Christ is buried in the Gulf of Mexico," I interjected.

"Where are you from?" Hilary asked. "Sedona, Arizona?"

"Banff, in Canada," I said. "*I liked you in that movie,*" I tried to say but the words came out garbled.

"What?" she asked.

Then, I looked into the hallway where Zach, the male attendant, was standing. His hair stood up around his head like a halo and I knew instinctively it was wrong to see that. I closed my eyes. When I reopened them, he was walking in. His hair was flat, but his third eye was a piece of black flint in the middle of his forehead. It had jagged edges and was raised a bit from his forehead, almost like it was a mole. I did not know if it was good or bad to see this. I could not differentiate.

He came in and looked at Bobby and John. "Hey, Barry and Jerry—you guys need to get down to the third floor for your treatments. It's almost time."

I looked at them. This time the scene was different. It was in color and they looked different. Oh! I see. They had morphed into what they were in reality in this dimension to everyone else. Otherwise, who would believe me when they asked me who I was talking to and meeting in this ward? If I told them who I'd been smoking with, then they'd really think I was crazy. Their secrets were safe with me. I panned the room and saw that they had all morphed—Nelson, Robin, Marilyn, David, Barbra, Houdini, Hilary. All had morphed into today's bodies.

Zach read from his list. "Dickey (aka Nelson Mandela), you have relatives in the waiting area. Better hustle. I think there is pie involved. Apple. Save me a slice, brother, will ya?

"Um. Let's see Lynn (Marilyn). You have an appointment with Dr. Spectrus in twenty minutes. Piper, Mandy called and can't see you till tomorrow. Buster and Gerald, you need your medication. See Paige about that, she's got it at the nurses' station. And, the rest of you, we have a movie getting ready to start in the lounge. So, if you want to watch it, it starts in fifteen minutes."

I tried to figure out the rest of their names. But, it all confused me. I could not keep track of it. My belly dropped and felt sick when he told me that Mandy would not visit. I longed for her to come and for me to tell her what amazing things were happening. Finding the cure for paralysis was going to be something. I was glad to help. I was also glad to eat the snake, to eat my fear and poop it out so that humankind could progress. God had chosen me to get this message to the world as well as some of the others. Quite the womanifesto. I just hated that I had to end up in a hospital to meet these celebrities who would help. But, I guessed this was the only way to effect change. My body and mind and spirit felt a hundred years old, like an ancient tree still living long after the will to survive the seasons had passed—but somebody had to endure it, I surmised. Somebody had to endure the pain to bring the pleasure of a cure. So, it was me. I would eat the snake to create the cure. What form this snake would take, I did not know. I just knew that Rose was in her room and I needed a shower and that glass case was sitting on her bedstand. The special one was in there. I knew she would release it in the night and it would slide up into my bed and sink its teeth into my lower back and that it would be the scariest thing I would ever endure. I knew I had to do this and it was okay. It was okay, okay, okay, because thousands of people would reap the reward. Conjugate the snake. Find the cure.

If Joan of Arc would just come, I would feel more at ease. I needed a guide, a role model, someone to ask a series of questions. I knew when she went to Orleans, she was afraid. Hell, I would be afraid if God dropped a sword from the sky and asked me to lead the French against the English. Callings were different then. Today, they happened in mental wards.

Chapter 6

Blue Ridge basketball was classified as one of the most competitive smaller Division I schools in the country. We weren't as well known as the Tennessees or UVAs or Stanfords, but our schedule was just as rigorous. The program was in a rebuilding year and that meant that I might see some playing time. What underscored this new year was some seasoned athletes, a seasoned coach, but a new method. We were to repeat every drill, every day, till we got it into our long-term muscle memory. This also meant that we were expected to come in with a selected partner during off hours and shoot hundreds of free throws and practice rapid-fire shooting. Kissie Martin was given the key to the back gym and all we had to do was go get it from her and we were in. We had to sign in and sign out and coach left us a CD player and a CD recorded at a game that made noise in the gym like you were in a real game.

Most everyone tried to get in between four p.m. and nine p.m., but I had signed up for a poetry class that was only taught until near-ly ten p.m. At first, no one wanted to go with me because it was late, but being the consummate flirt that I am, I asked Mandy Weaver if she would come on Thursday nights and I promised I wouldn't try and kiss her. I had been pursuing her hard since our ping party but to no avail. Even, after our trip up Route 20, she acted like I was low woman on the totem pole, like seniors were supposed to act toward frosh like me.

Still, I resigned myself to overtly flirting every chance I got. "So, Mandy, want to go to the movies?" I'd say, walking by her after prac-tice. She'd tell me to go smoke it out of my ears in a nice kind of way but I'd just laugh it off over my shoulder and keep up the pursuit. She was a hard nut to crack. I was a hard nut to crack.

Wednesday's preseason practice was going inordinately slow and Saneha Jones played with such a sassy attitude that I thought Coach Potter might self-combust from holding in an F-you or two. For thirty minutes, Saneha had not listened to a word anyone said and then one time just walked off the court to get water without asking permission. This was an act of anarchy and all of us knew that Coach Potter was watching every tone, every nuance, every dumb-ass thing Saneha did. We all knew she was cooking something up in her head for us to do as a team that would make us all throw up. Feeling the outcome already, I nodded to Jessie Holmstead to see if she saw what I saw. She nodded back and put her hands on her knees. Teeter rolled her eyes at me and I winked at her. Kara got into the point position and then out of the blue started to talk to Saneha like she was not in the gym.

"Getting on everyone's nerves, Sa-ne-hah," she said under her breath. "Needs to get her sassy act off the basketball stage and come up with a new theme."

Kara was a theater major and I liked her style. Her dribbling, she said one time, was like iambic pentameter. No one knew what that meant, but she could dribble the hell out of the basketball. Stand-ing just to the right of her in a three spot was another freshman, like me, Paulie Tomlinson. She echoed Kara's words. "New theme,

Sa-ne-hah."

Then all at once we began to say things like, "Come on, Saneha. Let's go. Come on. Let's do this together. Come on; get the lead out of your feet." Theonia said get it out of her ass, but no one heard that but Mandy Weaver and me. I had shuffled down to the baseline to stand next to Mandy. Glancing at Someday who was being scratched by Coach Dupont, I decided to get up my nerve.

"What are you doing tomorrow night?" I asked suddenly. I put my hands on my knees and looked at the score clock. We had two more minutes in this offensive position.

"I don't know. Writing a paper for a book I was supposed to read," she responded.

We didn't look at each other. I looked at Teeter and she grinned her toothy grin at me. There was still some Saneha tension and Coach Potter and then Coach DuPont were writing some stuff on their respective clipboards and comparing positions and plays. Coach Potter looked at Mandy for a split second and for a moment it made me feel weird. Why I wasn't sure.

"You want to come up here and help me shoot after my poetry class? It's late but I could help you with your paper. English is one of my better subjects. I aced every class in high school because one of my parents used to be a librarian. What's the book?"

Teeter moved into our spot to chat. *Not now, Teeter.* I did my frowny face at her and she sidled back up to Natalie Wingfield. Then she mouthed: RADONKULOUS. Kara began to dribble between her legs and then threw it around her waist to Theonia.

"*The Great Gatsby.*" She looked at me, finally.

"Jesus Christ, Mandy! You haven't read *The Great Gatsby?* That's standard English for high school juniors everywhere. I can tell you all about it. Hell, I probably have something already written in my iBook about it. What do you say? For a hundred free throws I can tell you what East Egg and West Egg mean and how fertile dreams fall short in the ideologies of men and minds."

"Piper, you're weird." It came from Nikki Jackson who was underneath the basket flipping a basketball around and around her waist.

"I know," I said, confidently. "Isn't it great."

Mandy looked at me as Coach Potter and Coach DuPont finished their secret coach chat. "I will meet you in the back gym at ten fifteen. Don't be late."

"Sweet. I will bring my computer and my copy of *Gatsby*. We can hack something out in twenty minutes." I looked at Teeter. She rolled her white eyes and picked at her wig while she did it. She knew I liked her.

"I'd rather do it on my own, thanks." She moved away from me and into position to hear what Coach Potter was about to announce.

Coach Potter threw her clipboard on the ground and the abominable snow coach came through loud and clear. "Everyone on the line except for Saneha. Now!" Uh-oh. We were in trouble, again.

We flew to the end line and we ran three suicides in a row. No stopping. Nikki Jackson led us and every time she passed Saneha she pointed at her like she was going to get it. How she could even get her pointer up was beyond me. All of us sucked wind at the end and then Coach Potter had Coach DuPont finish practice on account of her having to have a chat with Saneha in private.

"All right, girls. Get into position to run the Gold offense. I need the five blue shirts up here and the white shirts on D. Let's go. Get there. We don't have much time and we need to get in shape for Western Kentucky scrimmage. That's only ten days away girls. We have a lot to run through." He suddenly pointed at me. "Piper?"

"Yeah!" I ran up to him breathy, nervous.

"You need to move your feet on defense better. If you're going to step in for Saneha when she's like this, then you're going to need to move your feet better. Now, you're not as fast as Saneha, but you have better intuition about where to be. That's how you got here on scholarship. You have good court sense. Even still, you need to move your feet. Got it?"

"Yes, Coach. I'll work on it," I said.

"Good." He blew the whistle and put the ball in play. "I want the ball to be passed at least six times before anyone thinks about a shot. Go."

For the next hour and a half, we went over the Gold offense. Kara stumbled with the ball and shook her head and was pulled out for doing so. Natalie Wingfield arced in four three-pointers out of six attempts. Coach DuPont was elated and told her so. Mandy did her duty underneath the basket and when she got the ball, she posted up and went up strong, left then right, and then in the center with a soft hook shot. Teeter muscled everyone around and knocked almost everyone back on her ass before Coach told her to cut it out. She laughed and he turned and giggled at Kissie.

Coach Potter returned to the gym without Saneha. We all looked at each other in dismay and then continued our motion offense and then broke out into a three on two, two on one full court swing. It ended our practice.

We proceeded to the locker room to find Saneha's locker cleaned out. No one said a word. Someday lay down beside my locker while I changed into some jeans and a T-shirt. When I clipped the leash on her and headed out ten minutes later, I noticed Mandy and Coach Potter talking to each other in the dimly lit hallway near the coaches' office. I wasn't sure but I thought Mandy told Potter that Saneha would come back. Potter stood too close to her, I thought. My stomach dropped and Someday and I pushed through the double doors.

We drove up Route 20 and around my favorite bend while I drank three cold Miller Lites. Someday rested her head on the window and her ears flapped in the wind of the Blue Ridge Mountain air. I laid my hand on her back to comfort her, but it was really me who needed it more. When we got back to my apartment, I walked her across the footbridge to Monroe Park and we watched a wonderland of stars while she laid at my feet.

At 10:10 the next night, Someday and I showed up at the gym to meet Mandy Weaver to practice shooting and footwork. Running at the speed of sound, I heard clanging from the back of the Christian

Sydnor Hall but did not lurk around to find from where it issued. The clanging noises came and went and I dismissed them like gnats flickering into my vision. Wiped them out of the air. When I did this, most times, the noises stopped.

"Hey." Mandy Weaver rode up on her bike.

"You need a basket," I said.

"For what," she got off.

"Your bike. You need a basket for the front."

"Shut up. Teeter's right. You are radonkulous. You ready to practice some shooting?"

"You ready for me to kick your ass?"

"Piper, I outweigh you by fifty pounds. I don't think you'll be the one kicking ass."

"I'm scrappy, you know." I helped her with her bag and pushed her bike next to the gym door. "Did you bring the book?"

"No, I'm just going to work on it when I get back to my dorm."

"Twenty dollars and four margaritas, I can write that paper for you and you can get an A."

"That's just it. I don't want you to write it for me. Then it's like cheating. I don't want to cheat." Mandy slid the key into the door.

I grabbed her wrist.

She looked at me, incredulous at my flirty maneuvering. "Do you think this is good, your grabbing my wrist like that? And, by the way, do you always bring your dog everywhere you go?" She looked at Someday who was lying on the ground.

"I'm doing a report on the radius and ulna and wanted to get an empirical measure on yours. Do you mind? And, yes, my dog goes with me just about everywhere."

"Are you some sort of weird brainiac? What are you talking about?"

"Nothing." I heard the clanging and let go. "Do you want to get a beer after we shoot around?" The windy air swirled up between us and the light from the gym made the outline of Mandy's head glow, luminous, almost.

"Get in there, Piper. You are the biggest flirt I've ever seen. What do you want to work on?" We walked over the threshold of the door and almost immediately we began to stretch our arms and legs.

"Rapid fire. My feet. And the way to your heart."

"Well, I can help you with the first two. But my heart is closed right now for business. It's been that way since last spring and I like it that way."

"What? Did some girl break your heart?"

"Yeah. I guess you could say that."

"Who was she? Shall I put some chinks in her armor for you? Would that make you feel better? How about I write her a scathing letter and attach a picture of you and me kissing by Noon Bridge. Have you ever been to Jean Noon Bridge?"

"No." She dribbled the basketball and shot it on the inside, twice from the right and then twice from the left.

"Jean Noon was some big suffragette in the early twentieth century. They named the bridge after her because she crossed it a thousand times on her pilgrimages to Washington, D.C., and New York. She lived near Roanoke I think. But, she loved the bridge. When she died, they named it after her."

"Sounds like you read too much. Don't tell me now you know everything about Greek mythology and the history of the entire world."

"Well, I don't know anything about the history of the entire world. But, I do know a bit about Greek mythology. I'm writing it all down in my womanifesto."

"Shut up and shoot."

"Okay. But one thing."

"What?"

"I'm going to kick your ass!" With that I hunkered down and drove to the basket and shot a fadeaway jumper. Swish. Two points. She threw the ball back to me and I did a fake step to the right, then the left, then just pulled up and shot from twenty-five feet away. Beautiful arc. Swish.

"You're pretty good, you know," Mandy said as I tossed the ball to her. "Coach DuPont is right, though. You need to work on your three-point shooting. Get the ball off your shoulder. You need to beef those shoulders up."

"I know. I need to hit the weight room more. Here, you take the right side and I'll feed you the ball." She moved to the right and I began to chest pass the ball to her and rebound as well. "Tell me about yourself, Weaver." I ran for a loose ball and passed it to her.

"What do you want to know?" She shot the ball. Swish. Right through.

"Nice shot. I don't know. Anything." I fed her the ball again.

She dribbled a few times. "Well, I'm studying to be a Special Ed teacher. I'm learning the ins and outs of IEPs and educational plans as well as how to create a lesson. I didn't realize teachers' jobs were so difficult. I just thought they sat up in the front of the class behind the podium and read from a lesson plan book. I had no idea it was so hard."

I stopped, grabbed a water bottle from a nearby bench, and relaced my left sneaker. The stands were pulled taut against the gym walls and there were only two lights on above the far end basket where we were shooting. I heard her shoes squeak on the floor behind me. "Teaching is the hardest job in the world. Nobody told you that in school, Weaver?" I twirled the ball on my middle finger in front of her. "Teachers are the lowest on the pay totem pole and we expect the most out of them. The ultimate freaking paradox, wouldn't you say?"

"Yeah. I haven't agreed with most anything you've said up until now."

"Kiss me then and I'll tell you a story about a teacher," I said and winked at her. The sweat was pouring from our bodies and the air was thick and sexy. At least I thought it was thick and sexy.

"Why don't you just give me the story, oh-flirty-one?" She got some of her own water from her backpack. "Let's stretch out over here."

At the top of the key, just above the foul line around the blue painted arc, Mandy sat down and spread her legs and I mirrored her with a thud.

I began. "The woman who helped raise me was with a school teacher a long time ago . . ."

"How long?"

"I don't know. Maybe eight or nine years back, maybe ten."

"She was with a woman?"

"Yes. Her name was Frankie Bourdon. She was a phys. ed. teacher at Louisa High School near Richmond. They met at a pivotal time in both their lives. Vera, my guardian if you will, was a staunch-ass Republican and her girlfriend was a Democrat fighting to get the gay agenda into the classroom as a part of sex education."

"No shit, really?"

"Yep. She was on this crusade to just open the dialogue. That's all she wanted and she did everything she could to try and make it happen, including taking her appeal to the local school board. Vera told her she'd get squashed like a bug—"

"Did she?" Mandy handed me her water bottle.

"Wouldn't you want to know." I laughed then I took a sip and told her more about Vera.

"She sounds like she's a right-on kinda guardian." Mandy stretched down across the floor and laid on her back. Excellent.

I lay on my side and continued my story. "She took a risk. Vera took a risk to break all the rules to see who she loved the most and Vera didn't know how to break rules. She was a librarian, for God's sake. Librarians just know how to sit two to a table and stack and reshelve books."

"That's not all . . . shut up."

"You shut up," I said back. "It's a long story. Do you really want to know more?"

"Keep going. I just need to write an essay on *The Great Gatsby* by eight a.m."

"All that story is about is wanting something from the past that you can't reclaim, no matter how you try and recreate it."

"What do you mean, Piper?"

"Gatsby's this nouveau riche on Long Island who captured this chick's heart eight years back. The love affair ended went he went off to war. When he got back he spent his whole life creating what he thought she might want to get back a piece of the love they had before they were separated. He made big money as a criminal then built this huge house across from her house on Manhasset Bay on Long Island. He orchestrated the biggest way to woo a woman back in all of twentieth-century American literature."

Mandy sat up, "What happened? Did she get back with him?"

"For a bit . . . but then she went back to her husband. Gatsby until his death was dreaming that she'd come back again. The age of illusionment . . . even the Great Houdini couldn't have figured out that kind of love. Know what I mean?"

She looked at me. "It sounds like she broke his heart—"

"He broke his own through trying to recapture something that was long gone. People do it all the time. Girlfriends break up and then they can't get through the first night before they're calling her back wanting one last night together. Then they break up two months later because the best friend of the girlfriend is now in prime position to be the one."

"How did you become such a philosopher, Plato?"

"I prefer Einstein, Thoreau and Emerson, thank you."

"I prefer Navratilova, Hamm and King." Mandy lay back down.

"Martin Luther King?"

"No, stupid, Billie Jean. Talk about someone who risked it all."

"Mia Hamm?"

"Duh?"

"Okay. Just checking." We both laughed and I rolled over and put my hand on her forearm. It was sinewy and beaded with sweat. I could feel my heart vibrating my whole body. She let me keep my hand there. Should I keep talking? Perhaps Transcendentalism? Moliere? No. Too deep. Rilke. No. Still too deep. Emerson? Shakespeare? Mandy put her left arm to her left cheek to wipe some sweat away. I didn't move but watched.

Then, I quoted, "'O that I were a glove upon that hand that I might touch that cheek.' *Romeo and Juliet*, Act three, scene two."

"Kiss me, Piper."

That's all I needed.

When I put my lips to hers, I thought it would be the great awakening, but we clacked teeth and started to laugh. I hadn't even tried to separate her lips before I was pulled away by the numbing jolt that had us giggling and Mandy rolling to the side.

"No, come back here. That was horrible. Not romantic at all. I'd say more like tooth wrestling for the lip smackdown. Let's try it again, Weaver. Come on."

Then, she rolled over on top of me. Her whole torso was on top of my torso—her western hemisphere meeting my eastern hemisphere. Our sweaty legs intertwined and she put her lips on mine and my vagina contracted the way my lips intermingled with hers. At first, I tried to pay attention to how my top lip was interacting with her top lip, then down to her bottom lip. I held my eyes open, looking at her cheek bones, her closed eyes and her delicate nose dance around my lips. She pulled away and peeked at me. We smiled at the same time and then she kissed me again. This time, however, I closed my eyes and let my brain shut the hell up and let my body do the thinking. My body was much smarter. From the top of my head, an electric conduit came alive and the meridian lines on my body were re-engineered into a widening, a stretching that became three-dimensional, the energy and the heat and the sweat oils made me transcend out of my body into a sudden nothingness, both pregnant and empty. I was awareness, nothing more. And all because this hot basketball chick was swabbing my tongue with her tongue. Slow, then she would moan. Oh my! What a moan! And then she would find a point in my mouth with her tongue and moan some more. We were creating a sweaty cocoon, streamlined in our sweaty slickness and more breathless than if I'd been doing three suicides in a row. I sucked in air, it rotated between us. She pulled away and sucked in air. My hips arched up into hers and hers pressed down into mine. Magnificent sweaty oils leaked uncontrollably from between my legs and ran down my thighs. Arching, breathing, sweating, kissing, licking, touching. Then she touched the bridge of my neck between my chin and my lower neck. She touched it with her fingers and then with her lips. It burned. I shot up like a flame.

"Mandy—" I said. "No one has ever kissed me there before."

"Where? Here? On your neck? This spot . . ." She kissed me there again.

"Yes. Yes." I was vibrating all over, quivering.

"This place is a good spot. It's like a bridge between your head and your heart."

"I never thought of it that way." I pulled her into my arms and held her. Her head rested for a moment on my shoulder.

"You, you the crazy philosopher. I would think that you would know even that."

"No, but you can kiss this bridge anytime you want, Mandy Weaver." I pointed to it and she kissed it again, swathing her tongue across my chin down the arches across the esophagus to the pool of sweat lodged in between the base of my neck and the clavicle. The round dip. She left her tongue there for a moment and I came suddenly, with such surprise inside of my legs.

Rapture.

Chapter 7

At the Veterans Hospital in Richmond, my grandfather lay in his bed gnarled and unshaven and shallow in his breathing. He was the man who had driven me straight to Canada when I was just twelve years old. He had given up on me and I had given up on him. Jack Daniels, Budweiser and NASCAR had run his life for most of his life.

He didn't have any time for a little girl like me, especially after what he'd done to my family. He'd killed them all in his own drunkenness at an intersection where he fumbled for an extra sip of beer while running a red light. He was ejected because he didn't have on a seatbelt. My mother and father and brother were killed instantly on impact. Victor walked away from the accident, through the woods, and meandered to a Patient First he saw on the side of the road. He told them he'd fallen down on the pier when he was fishing and had cut his face on a protruding nail on the dock. He got a ride home that night, picked me up and took me to Curbside Café where he proceeded to tell me that Mom and Dad and Jack had gone on a little trip and would be back in the morning.

When the police told me the next day what had happened, everything in me went numb—numb for three years. I was just nine years old. Mom and Dad and Jack had left me with my dumbass grandfather and Someday—the lame dog. It was too much to bear. I didn't realize till much later that no one knew my grandfather had driven the truck that night. They must have thought my father was driving the truck since it was his. The reason I knew was because when I was left behind with Someday, I saw my grandfather grab a beer from the fridge and get into the driver's seat of the truck. Watching it all from the bay window of my house, it was surreal—all so surreal.

During the third week of October, Mandy came with me to Richmond to see him. Teeter had relatives in Richmond, too, so she and Kissie Martin followed in their hooptie behind us. We were all to go out dancing at Shockoe Sally's Bar and Grill after our respective visits. Kissie said she liked the barbecue and Teeter liked to boogie to the gay disco it turned into after dark.

Next to the bar was a coffee and bookshop Vera had told me about, Fountain Bookstore. The inside of any bookstore always made me feel like I was in one of C.S. Lewis's books. Picking up anything and reading and staring and procuring information. I loved it. I told Vera I would pick up a copy of Dylan Thomas's works and a psychology book by Jean Bolen called the *Tao of Psychology*. Vera had told me that it was a book to change your life, like anything we'd shared by John Irving. I promised her I'd get them both. Of course, I wasn't sure when I'd have time to read them.

Einstein's theory of relativity had been bugging me lately and I had begun journaling in earnest about his theory and some of Immanuel Kant's theories on how the universe had conceived itself. William James filtered his own psychological theories, so I found myself Googling him and a myriad of others. The connections I was seeing between the scientists and poets and philosophers was some intense stuff. If you could stamp the universe with a brilliant idea that you fetched out of the dark, fleshy confines of your brain and prove it as it related to the philosophies and empirical data and real data of who was and who once was—like Einstein or even Jesus, well, then let the neurons and dendrites have a firing party, because I wanted to know how to change the world, by expunging one fucked up thing at a time—pedophiles and rapists and child molesters and misogynists all at once. Simply stated, hand the key over to the women. They'd clean up the mess. Our best role model? The Virgin Mary of course. I had begun to read the Bible, too. Jenny and Andrea said I had to. It was the most important piece of weaponry on the face of the earth.

I wasn't sure why I was coming to see the man who had killed my entire family. But, his sister had contacted me through Vera and Jenny and Andrea because he was not well and had asked about me. So, reluctantly, I made the trip to Richmond just three weeks after I began falling in love with Mandy Weaver.

Driving from Charlottesville to Richmond was an easy drive. We ambled in my truck through Albemarle, Fluvanna, Louisa and Goochland Counties before I made some turns in and around Route 522 and up to Carver Middle School to show Mandy the rural apartment complex in Goochland County where I'd been saved by my foster parents one fall six years earlier.

Teeter kept honking her horn because I guess she thought I was going too slowly. I gave her the finger, lit a cigarette and rolled my window down. I loved the taste of a Marlboro Light cigarette, especially with a cold beer. I was the only smoker on the team except for Jessie Holmstead who smoked them with me on my small deck drinking margaritas. "Don't tell anyone," she'd say to me. I winked at her and kept it a secret but told her if her parents came around I might give her up if she took my potential starting position. She told me to kiss her ass and I did.

"What happened?" Mandy asked, drinking her beer.

"He was just slam drunk all the time," I said. "Hand me one." Mandy opened a beer and handed it over to me. I put it between my legs.

"Piper, you should slow up on the beer before going to see him."

"Well, that's ironic, isn't it? Slow up on beer. Hell, I think we should stop and get us an IV of vodka before going to the hospital."

"Well, your aunt will be there, right? You want to make a good impression on her."

"The only person I want to make a good impression on is you, Mandy Dream Weaver."

"You are, silly." She put her hand on my thigh and I grabbed it with my hand.

"I like you. You're the craziest girl I've ever known."

"Crazy about you," I said.

"We are sounding very sappy." She swallowed her beer and turned up the radio.

"Sappy is good. What's wrong with sappy? Here—" I pointed. "Let's pull over here. I want to show you something. I'll get Someday on a leash and you grab a couple of beers."

"Teeter is going to think you're bowing out of going to see your grandfather."

"No she's not. She and Kissie can go on their merry way. Unless they want to go deep into the woods with me and you."

I pulled the car into the old cul-de-sac where I had grown up shooting basketball. The rusted hoop was still there but had no chain netting. The overgrowth on the woods behind it seemed older and thicker. The apartments were all the same. Old brick tied together with flat boarding and every screen door looked melancholy from years of slamming and scratching.

Someday got out of the car and I gave her water. I trickled some on her head and neck to cool her off and then kissed her on her snout and then in between her eyes. "Good girl."

Mandy put her hands on her hips and looked at the hoop. I fingered the cross on my neck and thought of my mother—the cross was hers. Something I had nearly thrown away once. The time I gave up on God.

"What are you mumbling?" Mandy asked.

"What?"

"You said you threw the loss at God?"

Kissie, the basketball manager, got out of the passenger side of Teeter's car. She must have been five foot three and 275 pounds, easily. She loved barbecue and her hair extensions had small shelled beads in them.

She slammed the door. "Piper, where in the hell are we? You've been running around these last few streets like you're the Pope coming home. I'm surprised you're not waving out dat truck window at the squirrels and the groundhogs and the damn rabbits for God's sake. You going slower than Teeter does taking a test on one plus one equals two."

Teeter slammed her door. "Kissie, I heard that. You better watch your slappy mouth, girl or I'll make you a one plus one double sandwich." She folded both fists and hooved them up in the air like she was going to fight.

"Teeter," Kissie remarked.

"What?" Teeter put her arms by her side.

"Shut your gay mouth!"

"Hey, I take offense to that," Mandy said.

Kissie looked at her. "Your mouth is really gay, so I wouldn't be saying nothing, Mandolin."

I laughed. "Both of you shut up. I just want to show her something really quickly. Okay? Do you want to wait or do you need to get to your aunt's house before your pants catch on fire from riding so low in that hooptie of yours?"

"This is my baby—"

Kissie squirmed a bit. "Get your dog away from me. He stinks. Gawd."

"She's old, Kissie," I said. "Give her a break. She's a good girl. She won't bite you."

"That's what my Uncle Gerald said right before the cat bit half his eye out. Good kitty, then, *r-r-r-r-eeeee-rrrnh.*" She raked her hands in the air. "Then he was Glass-Eyed Gerald from then on."

Teeter got back in the car. "Kissie, come on. That dog don't worry me none. She's okay. You two go make out in the woods and then hurry back. I want to see my radonkulous aunt. Lord, she'd kill me if she heard me say that."

"I didn't say anything. Come on," I said to Mandy. "Let me show you my old fort. We can kill some time in the woods. Plus, I do want to make out with you."

Ambling down the back of the street, we found the beaten path I used to find every day I ran away with my dog to solitude.

Mandy said, "If we keep kissing, I think someone is just going to find a bunch of bones and clothes in the woods—"

"Why do you say that?" I asked.

"Because we are both melting away with all this crazy fire between us. We're going to be found draped across one another in a pool of something, I don't know what."

"A pool of lips and hips and ticks—"

"Ticks?"

"Yeah, come here. You've got one on your back." I reached to grab it off her T-shirt.

"Ooh, get it. I hate those things worse than mosquitos."

"Quit moving around and I'll get it, you sissy." I reached again and grabbed the tick and threw it on the ground. "Ticks are a curious beast, you know. They wait their whole entire lives for the right time to jump from a leaf or a vine or a limb. They stay patient and wait, wait, wait and then . . ." I grabbed Mandy's strong shoulders. "Then, they grab onto the unsuspecting sucker and," I turned her toward me, "and sink into them." I kissed her vehemently and then heard a loud clanging from the old rickety pier fifty yards away. It was so close.

I pulled away from her. She looked cross-eyed. "Did you hear that noise?"

"What noise? You scare me sometimes, Piper."

"Nothing. Sometimes I hear this clanging and I'm not sure if it's in my head or if it's real. Know what I mean?"

"Well, you need to get your head examined then."

I put my hands to my head and felt around. "It feels pretty good, here—" I grabbed her hands and put them on mine. "Feel it. What do you feel?"

She stopped me from fooling around. "You have a gift, Piper. You say things and make things up and sing stupid rhymes. And, they're really stupid. But, they're smart and funny." She held me with her eyes. I thought my knees might buckle. She seemed to get taller. "You drive me crazy with all your idiot philosophies and what-you-call musings. I don't understand you sometimes but you're fun. That's all I can manage sometimes with you. Just the fun."

"Well, Ms. Weaver, that's the spirit! You're about to have the ride of your life. Someday and me are going to take you to all sorts of places. And, if we can't drive there, then I'll make them up. We'll wrestle with the spirits, walk along railroad tracks, pick apples from rows of orchards, walk across lonely bridges, and kiss in broad daylight on the downtown mall. The places can be exotic right here." I placed my hand on her heart. She put hers on mine. "There's a rainforest of emotion right here in this place beneath your breastbone. And Someday likes you, by the way. I could tell right away when she put her bad leg on your thigh. She's no dummy. She knows a good-looking girl when she sees one."

I stopped dead in my tracks as if struck by an old apparition; a specter had lifted in the twilight. My old fort just opened up before us. The side boards had caved in and the floorboard had rusty nails shooting up along the sides. Ivy grew in and around the cornered edges and there was moss all along the sides. There were some old papers and books and magazines underneath the dried leaves. The loneliness of the place created a melancholy that made me reach for my throat and chest. Then a longing came from my belly when I turned to face the stretch of open air and land that led to the river and the pier where my mom and dad and brother used to fish on Sundays. It was the place where we found Someday.

"My dog saved me here one night a long time ago," I said. I looked at my old dog. "Good girl." She wagged her tail and went ahead on the pathway.

"How in the world did she do that with that paw and all?"

"Well, she may seem slow, but that night when this crazy slobbery guy was trying to molest me, Someday tore his leg to pieces.

I ran to safety. I didn't see it. I heard her squeal and whimper and call to me. And I didn't realize till later that it made her deaf in her right ear. He tried to kick her head in. It was the Fourth of July and no one could hear me yelling. Someday went missing for three days after that. It was the saddest three days of my life till we found her in the pound."

"We?" Mandy asked.

"Me and Andrea. She and Jenny helped me look and one of the last places was the animal shelter. That was the beginning of how I got away from Victor. That sorry-ass snake tried to keep me around. Then after a week of talking, he gave me up to Jenny and Andrea and Vera. He told them he'd be happy to sign me over and to keep me and my stinky-ass dog away from him forever."

"Why in the world would you even think about visiting him, then?" Mandy took my hand.

"He asked to see me. He's dying. Sometimes when people are dying you do shit you don't feel like doing. Going to see him is something he wants—not me."

"You're right sometimes we do shit we don't feel like doing."

From the bushes we heard Kissie yell, "And this is the shit we don't feel like doing. Get your lazy asses back up here and let's get going. Teeter has eaten all the Slim Jims and is into the Cheetos. If you all hang around down there, we might have some serious gas running down the court on Monday. Hurry up. Teeter gets the worst gas in the world and I'm the one riding with her. If the wind breaks, it isn't going to be because I have my window rolled down. Hurry. Hurry."

"We're coming," Mandy yelled up.

"Will you come back here with me and Someday?" I asked.

"Sure. But I don't see why you would want to come back here. There are so many bad memories."

"The good ones are over here." I proceeded up the small ravine and over it. Then I pointed to the rickety pier and the spread of beach and the bridge that connected the river to the other side across railroad tracks. "My mother and I used to throw rocks in the river while my dad and Jack fished from the pier. Sometimes Jack and me would run back and forth across the bridge with Someday chasing us. Butterflies everywhere. Jack would hug Someday around her whole body and slap my ankles with switches he pulled off the forsythia. See, these are good memories."

"Funny how the good memories are betrayed by the bad ones." Mandy said.

"Who's the philosopher now, Mandy Weaver?"

"Piper Cliff, kiss me and shut your yap about this stuff. You're making me sad." She pecked my lips, slapped my butt, and then ran with Someday back down the path.

I called after her, "The only way you'll ever truly be sad, Mandy Weaver is if you stop kissing me! Stick that in your snickety snack and smoke it."

"I'm not going to stop kissing you, you crazy girl!"

Stopping at Lucky's convenience store, I got a twelve-pack of Miller Lite for the cooler and then explained to Teeter and Kissie how to get to Route 288 to the Southside and we all agreed to meet later at Shockoe Sally's. Kissie told us not to be late because she wasn't going to be stuck trying to talk to the only straight girl in the bar, and she yelled, "I want to dance with some white girls!" When we asked her why she said, "Because black girls look extra good dancing with girls who don't know how to dance. It's like dancing with white men but not as bad." Mandy gave her the finger and I told her we'd be on time.

Smoking three cigarettes and downing three beers each, Mandy and I made it into Richmond across Belt Boulevard and to the Veterans Hospital. She told me twice to slow up on the beer, but I made it a point to change the CD and change the conversation. When we approached the simple, lonely, stone hospital building, my eyes felt like they couldn't stay focused on anything: not the road, not the building front, not the inside dash. My eyes began to dart here and there and my anxiety compressed into my chest and lungs. My thoughts acted like a sieve, they couldn't create or hold anything for more than a second or two. Flash: my brother. Flash: my mother. Flash: my father. Flash: my dog. Flash: my life as a young girl, lost. Flash: the colors changed to black and white—everything, even the stop sign had no red.

Once inside the hospital, I felt like I was spinning on a mandala wheel looking for my own epicenter. This was going to be tricky. I did not tell Mandy about the dizziness or the sudden change in color. I chalked it up to the six or seven beers I'd had since leaving Charlottesville.

A reticence enveloped Mandy as we walked in. I could feel it. She didn't want to be here. There were old farty men in outdated wheelchairs sitting stolid, vapid and vacant. Some stared, others mumbled. Two or three we passed reached out their hands like they needed something. An oily-looking man with long stringy hair grabbed my hand and abruptly asked me if Bobby Kennedy was coming to Luther Memorial.

He held onto me. "He's coming. I know he is. Told my little brother Robin that he was coming. Did you hear about the two girls murdered up in Spotwood County? Robin said that Bobby knew who did it."

I grabbed his hand. "What girls?"

"Come on Piper." Mandy walked ahead and grabbed my hand but I jerked away from her. Two nurses passed us without a passing glance.

"Wait. What girls?" I asked again.

"The two that was raped and murdered down by the James River. Took from their house in broad daylight. Double rainbow come out later and everyone knew they was dead. Bobby knows the whole story and is coming to Luther Memorial tonight to talk about it. Can you call my brother and tell him to come and get me? Did you see the rainbow?"

"No. What's your brother's name?" I asked.

Mandy leaned in. "Come on. The guy's mixed up. He doesn't know what he's talking about."

"I already told you. His name is Robin." He let go of my arm.

"Who are you?" He looked at Mandy.

Mandy shook her head and walked down toward the waiting area.

"What's Robin's number?" I asked. "I'll call him for you."

"Well, I thought you might know what his number was. They took everything away from me. I don't have my black book. My little black book with all the names." He looked at the blue, chipped wall and began chewing on his fingernails. "When they took that away, I lost everything."

"Does the nurse have your black book, maybe?" I questioned.

"They don't read the Bible here, Miss."

"What's your name sir?"

"My name is Harry Williams." He smiled his gappy smile.

"And, your brother is Robin?"

"Yes."

"Well, sir. I'll see what I can do to get a hold of your brother. Does he live in the Richmond area?"

"No. He lives in California. Either in Hollywood or somewhere near there."

"And you want him to come pick you up to go see Bobby?"

"Yes. Victor says that if he catches the red-eye that he can be here in time to give me a ride. I just want a ride." He whimpered, then started to cry.

"Victor?"

"Yeah. Victor Cliff. He's down in room forty-two. That guy has all the answers. He told me that the red-eye can get Robin here and that Barbra might sing one of her songs from that movie, *The Way We Were*."

Jesus H. Christ. What in the world? This guy was certifiable. I was caught in his vortex and Mandy had left me with him. Weird, though, because part of him, part of what he was saying, I believed.

"I'll talk to the nurse, okay?"

"Thank you. I just want a ride to the meeting. That's all. Bobby knows who took them girls and it will help the police catch him. Hurting little girls is the worst thing in the world, Miss. You understand? Do you *understand*?" His voice pitched higher.

"Sir, I do. I understand. I'll try and help. I want to help you."

"Thank you, Miss. Can you do one more thing? Stay here a minute more," he said, then reached for my hand and grabbed my index and middle finger.

"Yes sir. I can do that."

It wasn't hard to stay a minute more. The old man was confused but made some sense. Robin Williams. I laughed inside. How does one get Robin Williams on the phone? How does anyone get anyone famous on the phone? Untouchable. Famous people were untouchable, unreachable, like there were invisible barriers up all around them. The only famous person I'd ever met was the local weatherman in Banff who ended up getting fired after sleeping with a girl thirteen years younger than him and then stalking her till he was found one day passed out drunk in her rose bushes with his pants around his ankles. Creep. Now I was getting the creeps. The black and whiteness of my world began to wither back to color and my head felt less fuzzy.

Letting go of his hand, I touched his shoulder and went down to find Mandy and room forty-two. When I approached, I sensed more trepidation. She handed me a Coke and we walked in silence toward the man who had taken my whole life away—a man who, as intimated by Harry Williams down the hall, was the guy who had all the answers.

The nurse at the nurses' station pointed when we asked and we went around the bend into his sterile, simple hospital room.

There he was: Victor Cliff. It was the first time I'd laid eyes on him in over six years. His hip bones pointed up from underneath the sheets and his face was drawn in at his cheeks and his temple. He was wispy bald and his eyes were sunken in and hollow black. Lifting a Styrofoam cup to his mouth, he looked at me and did not know who I was. I regarded him. He regarded me. Uneasy with the pregnant pause, Mandy walked out of the room and left me there alone with my grandfather.

"Can I help you?" he asked.

"A long time ago you could have." I stepped closer. "It's Piper, Victor."

"Well, you're a lot taller now," he said putting his cup down and lifting the covers higher around him.

"You called and asked me to come."

"Yes. I called. Your hair is darker. You turned out to be right pretty. Wasn't sure what you'd turn out to look like when you was the little ugly duckling. Now look at you."

"Well, I guess I'll take that as a compliment."

"You should. Come closer. Sit down. There's a chair over there."

"I prefer to stand, thank you."

"Oh, I see. Not staying long?"

"Not sure of the point," I said nonchalantly.

He had pictures on his table but I did not recognize anyone. Folding my arms, I kept the emotional distance. I wanted to hold it in, keep it all bunched up and heaved into my chest like an accordion that couldn't unfold.

"I met your roommate outside," I finally said. "He's got some notion you know all the answers and he wants his brother—Robin Williams—to come and get him because Bobby Kennedy is going to speak about something. I don't know."

"Oh, Harry. Yeah, he's not running on all eight cylinders. I don't know if I have all the answers. But, I sure have been asking better questions. He mentioned something about that in his waking sleep this morning. He's upset about the double murder of those girls in Spotwood . . . I hear you're playing basketball at BRU. You must be pretty good?"

"Not too bad. Pretty good outside shot but I need to work on beefing up these skinny shoulders of mine."

He sat up in his bed and put his glasses on to see better. "I remember you and that ole dog shooting baskets on Stoney Creek till well after dark years ago. How's Someday? She still around?"

I ignored the question. "Are you dying?" It came out faster than I intended.

"Yes. I suppose we all are."

"Who's 'we'?"

"The whole world is terminal, little girl."

"Please don't call me that. And my dog is old but she's doing fine. She's sitting in the truck right now. As I remember you didn't care much for her."

There was a pause. "Well, I was pretty confused back then, you know. You don't want me to call you little girl or terminal?"

"What do you want from me, Victor? I don't have much time. My friends are expecting me . . ."

"You're right. People don't have time for the sick and dying. There's too much shopping and TV to watch. In your case basketball to play, I guess."

"Yeah. I guess you could say that."

"You got a fella at school yet?"

"A girl. I have a girl."

"Oh. I see. A girl. She treat you right?"

"What do you know about treating people?"

He shifted in his bed and looked out the window at a large birch tree. "Now, it looks like you're the one asking good questions. That's why I asked you to come, little girl." He said it again and I could feel my stomach tie up in knots. "I've got this cancer, you know, that's eating up my brain. I'm sure the kind of life I led was no help for those carcinogens hopping onto every one of my cells and partying down. You left me six years ago for a different life—pissed me off to no end that those girls took you away from here. I drank Jack Daniels straight for about eighteen months till I nearly killed myself falling out of a tree trying to put up one of your signs in that fort where you used to smoke all my cigarettes."

"You know about the cigarettes? I thought you were too drunk to notice." I leaned against the wall and checked my fingernails. Then I crossed my arms and waited for the next piece of information.

"Marlboro Lights. Even though drunk people are drunk, they still figure things out. At least the ones who don't black out."

This pissed me off. "As I recall, Victor, you were quite good at passing out and pissing all over yourself. Just about every day I got home from school. There you were. Lying in your own pee. Too lazy and drunk to get up—you know, this is useless. I have to go. I'm not sure why I am here. I feel funny and weird, all over. Mandy is waiting for me outside—"

"Mandy is your friend?"

"Bad question. She's my girlfriend. Anything else?"

"No. Will you come again?" He looked out the window to the space of trees and the Lee Bridge that crossed over the river. I didn't say a word but dropped my arms. A nurse walked in and tossed me a haughty look. She went to him and adjusted some instruments and then wrote something on a notepad. When she walked back by me, she showed me what she wrote:

He doesn't drink anymore. Keep your voice down next time.

"Kiss my ass!" I yelled to her as she walked out. She didn't turn around but Mandy came in to get me.

"Come on. Let's go. Hospitals give me the creeps . . . especially this one. It smells like old dusty people everywhere." Mandy pulled my arm.

"Victor. We're going. You've done what you've done. You know. I'll be bearing that cross for the rest of my life. Tell my folks and my brother when you get to heaven that I miss them very much. Oh. Darn. I almost forgot. You're not going to heaven. Silly me." It came out before I could stop it from coming. I walked out half glad I had said it.

"That was kind of mean," Mandy remarked.

"Fuck this place," I said. "I didn't need him then. I certainly don't need him now. Old fart can die in his own liquid shit for all I care."

Victor yelled, "Come back here. Please—"

Floating is what I did down that sterile hallway that smelled like old dusty ass. I went by the old Harry Williams who was isolated in that crazy brain of his.

"I don't think we can help you, Mr. Williams. But, you're right, Mr. Cliff has all the answers down there."

"What answers?" Mandy asked as we walked through the double doors.

"The answers to nothing, Mandy. It's all nothing, especially now. You ready to eat, drink, dance and forever be a fairy?"

"You're the fairy."

"I'm a fairy tale."

We jaunted to the truck. My dizziness had subsided but a stifled clanging noise came from near the Lee Bridge. Letting it go, I jumped into the truck with Mandy.

"Are you coming back here?" she asked as I put a cigarette to my mouth.

"Hell no. He's dying and wants some kind of last-minute forgiveness from me. I'm not giving him that satisfaction. I don't think it's in me." I drew in a long drag from my cigarette.

"But I thought you said he asked you to come here and that you were coming for that reason . . . you know, to forgive, maybe? I thought that was the general idea." Mandy opened a beer and handed it to me while I turned the ignition.

I threw my cigarette out the window and flashed my head around like a bad scene from the *Exorcist*. "Let me just tell you one time. Just one time. So listen good. You hear me?" I was yelling. "That son-of-a-bitch took everything from me and he almost succeeded in getting my dog put down at the local pound. So as far as I'm concerned that man can have his ass get boils all over him and he can lie in his fecal farting aroma and die the slowest death since Jesus Christ. He took everything away, all away—away, away, away . . ."

I could not stop saying the word. It was like my brain was on perpetual skip and it wouldn't stop. I put my hands to my lips to stop it but my mouth kept saying it. For three or four infernal minutes, I yelled the word *away*. I became so agitated and scared that I could not stop, so I jumped out of the truck and ran all the way to the Lee Bridge. I was cataleptically embarrassed and could not stop my mouth from saying the word *away*.

From the bridge, I observed the truck to see what Mandy was doing. Finally, I screamed the last away and Mandy got out.

"Shit." I said it hoping it wouldn't come in the same form "away" did. Mandy ran toward me, then slowed up at the edge of the bridge and the road.

"I came here to support you, Piper." She turned on her shoe. "That's it—to support you and now you're yelling at me. I didn't do anything to you—"

"Not yet—"

"Not yet? Not yet? Do you really think I'm going to do something to you like he did?"

"No." I was impish. "I just pushed it all in. I can't get it out of here." I pointed to my head. "Nor here." I put my hand on my heart. "It all comes up into my chest till I think I might choke sometimes from all of it. Sometimes I can't speak. It's like I've got something tied tight around my throat and I panic and it hurts. I miss them. I will spend my whole life missing them. Little girls aren't supposed to lose their brother, or their father, or their mother all at once. It's too much. It's still too much. I can hardly move sometimes because my body feels like it's pinched in pain and hollowness and melancholy and holy fucking fuck. All the time. Not just some of the time."

"Calm down, Piper."

"Calm down. You want me to calm down. You're kidding, right? How do you know? How do you know what it's like? That's the supportive fucking spirit. Who have you lost?"

"No one. Let's go then—"

"I'm sorry."

Mandy didn't look at me and got back in the truck and slammed the door, but it didn't shut. It got caught on the seatbelt buckle that was hanging outside the bottom frame and she slammed it three or four good slams till she realized what it was precluding her from shutting it. She groaned in agitation and frustration and when I started to laugh that pissed her off even more.

The nearby church bell tolled and suddenly I was upset that I upset her. We drove off to Shockoe Sally's, drinking gulps of beer in silence. The burning cigarette stayed near the cracked window of my truck and every now and again I would flick ashes off it in disgust out the window while trying to think of something that would help the situation. Our first fight at the close of seeing my dying grandfather wasn't so funny now. I tried to reach for her hand but she crossed her arms.

Peering at the Richmond skyline of skyscrapers, I could feel her falling away somewhere else, her sensual loving grip loosened. The dreaminess of Mandy Weaver faded, turning to a kind of vapidity, a flimsy film hanging in my mind. The images of recent first flirtings and first kissings were expunged by the gravity of yelling words that had cut into me and into her. They would tarnish us for a long time to come, like first fights tarnished any couple. You could never take the tarnish away. You could fight with parents and siblings and almost always return to normal. After fighting with a girl, nothing ever was the mystic same as it once was. This was a travesty of love that no one could figure the fuck out. Not even my mossy brain, my mossy brain, my mossy brain. Inside the repeat came again, like every movement I made now was a basketball drill gone infinite loop. Loop. Loop. Loop.

I flicked the cigarette out the window and pulled out another one and lit it. Without warning, I had this insane longing to just be back at home in Banff with Someday and to sleep with her while hearing Vera yelling out plausible answers to crossword puzzles to Andrea.

Chapter 8

At the bottom of the four lane Lee Bridge, which connected the southside of Richmond to the northside of Richmond and ran parallel to the railroad tracks from the Norfolk shipyard all the way to Missouri, was the famous historic district called Shockoe Bottom. Revolutionaries like Patrick Henry and Thomas Jefferson had made famous speeches in and around the cobblestone streets to change the way America would think then and now. At the edge of the James River, a farmer's market bustled during the day with rich people from the west end. And the clubs and restaurants were packed at night with thousands of college students from the two local universities: Virginia Commonwealth University and the University of Richmond—both in-state rivals of Blue Ridge University. Street urchins and hustlers and gangsters milled about in their respective venues three streets over and as the evening drew into night and then early morning, the three differing factions of people would integrate as the alcohol either strengthened or loosened attitudes. The tide of the commerce and trade aged the store owners and bar owners by twenty years. But, they stayed in it. Sometimes once you're in, you can never get out. Shockoe Sally's was the gay venue near the edge of the market and the corner bistro that doubled as the Fountain Bookstore I was supposed to check out.

"I'll meet you after I read *War and Peace* by Leo Tolstoy," I said.

Mandy put her hands in the air and walked into the bar. The *boom boom* seered through the air as she opened the door while pulling out her ID.

My eyes were riveted by the headlines of the *Richmond Times-Dispatch:* Spotwood Girls Found Dead Near Pebble Creek. Scanning the story, I learned that they were in the nude and near the underpass. Both had been strangled. I gripped my neck and put the paper down. I couldn't bear to read more. The guy at the VA had talked about how two double rainbows had come out the morning they found them. One girl was twelve; the other nine. Sisters. I wanted to throw up.

Walking down the aisle, I stopped in the poetry section and browsed the authors. Vera was hot for Walt Whitman, but I didn't feel like looking for "Song of Myself" right now. "Dirge of Myself" was more like it: something dark. Where was Sylvia Plath when you needed her. Then a young slender, dark, bookish woman with glasses came up: sultry.

"Can I help you find anything?" she asked.

I smiled and said, "My heart and soul." I swayed back a bit and felt my face get hot.

She pushed her glasses up and put her hands on her hips. "Well, let's see. For heart, you might want to read Edna St. Vincent Millay. She's down here." She pointed. "For soul, you might want to read Rilke or Rimbaud or Shelley. They're all here." She pointed to a stack below Millay.

"What about silly?" I asked.

"Dr. Seuss is in the children's section over there." She pointed while turning to face where the books stood covers out and at attention.

Then a man in a tweed suit and donning light-colored sunglasses came through the door and my bookstore friend hurried away toward him and began a chitchat. He kept his glasses on, which I thought strange. Then they both turned to look at me. The woman leaned in and mouthed what looked like a yes and then he put his hand on her shoulder and walked with her to the back of the store.

Browsing for a minute or two more, I found the book Vera wanted: *The Tao of Psychology* by Jean Bolen. Pulling out my money, I stopped by the register to wait for her to ring me up. When she returned, she had on sunglasses, too. Or, were they? The framework of the register and the back wall and the cups of pens and pencils and bookmarks were all in black and white.

"Bright in here, eh?" I said nervously. She was tall and her face was taut and weirdly looked like some movie star I couldn't make out.

"Is this the only book you want?" she asked.

"Do you think I need another one?"

"Well, perhaps. Did you look in the mind section?"

"The mind section?"

"You said you were looking for your heart and soul . . . but made no mention of your mind? Aren't you looking for that, too?" She smiled.

Paranoia was on me like a snake around my neck. "Okay?" My hands quivered and I put them deep in my jeans. Then my elbows shook. I took my hands out. I did not want to start repeating words in my mouth nor in my head.

She came out from behind the counter and walked me to another section. "Here, here's one you might like." She pulled a book from the shelf. "He's one of my favorite authors. It's called *Palms of the Holy*, by this famous priest: Gordon Robertson. It discusses the mapping of the minds of the saints and what they held in here—" She pointed to her head, "—and what they held in their hands, the palms of their hands and how they all interlocked one another symbolically and spiritually."

"Sounds heavy," I said.

She pushed her sunglasses to the top of her head and the pupils of her eyes vibrated as they dilated then contracted back again. "You seem like someone who can handle heavy reading."

I stepped back and glanced out the window to the clock: 9:22 on Saturday night in a city of angels I imagined. "Okay, it's a sale."

"You from Richmond?" she asked as she rang me up.

"Yes, but I'm a student at BRU . . ."

She put the books in a bag and sealed it shut. "BRU. So, you're up in Charlottesville. Pretty country up there. Here's my card. If you like this book, then go to our Web site and e-mail me and I'll send you some other recommendations."

"Maybe one day you will be able to recommend mine," I said, then looked down.

She placed the bag on the counter. "Oh! You're a writer, too?"

"Yes. I don't have anything published, but I'm keeping up the spirit of just doing it for doing its own sake. I think it has some good things in it: a womanifesto!"

"Well, keep it up. I'm sure you will make it someday."

"Wow, that's my dog's name . . . Someday—" I grabbed the bag of books and turned toward the door. "Thanks for your help! What's your name?"

"Hilary . . . yeah, no problem. That's a cool name for a dog."

"She's the greatest dog in the world," I said confidently. "I'm Piper . . . Piper Cliff."

"Well, Piper. I hope to see you on a back cover with your dog in the near future!"

I smiled at her and went through the door. It reminded me of an arbor, an archway of sorts, but I shook the image from my head.

Closing the door behind me, I got a chill from the October wind that rumpled the bag under my arm.

I saw the man in the sunglasses on the corner three blocks down. Ignoring him and the funny feeling in my stomach, I walked into a smoky Shockoe Sally's to join the basketball army of Teeter and Kissie and the funky mood I knew Mandy Weaver would be in.

Deep breath. Deep breath, I thought.

Mandy was playing pool with some older butch women, while Teeter and Kissie danced to the syncopation of the techno music. The thumping made my heart feel like it was going to beat right out of my chest, especially when I caught Mandy glancing at me while whispering in some girl's ear. She was testing my jealousy and was very much getting what she wanted. The girl was slender, sexy and hot. Fuck, I thought. Now was the time to get drunk off top-shelf margaritas. It was the best approach to the diabolical situation I had gotten myself into. But, what did I know. I was just some stupid basketball-playing jock at Blue Ridge University trying to get along.

"Hey there—" A gothic-looking freakshow sidled up to me. "I'm Poutina. I'm from Puerto Rico. Where are you from?"

"Canada," I said. I looked to Teeter who winked at me and kept gyrating like a belly dancer on crack.

"Canada. Where's Canada? Isn't that near the top of the world?"

Jesus Christ. "It's near Darfur in Africa."

"Who's a dark whore?"

"No," I said. "Darfur." I stepped back.

"Oh. You want to dance?"

"Sure, thanks. What's your name Poutanga?" I really shouldn't have been dithering around but didn't care.

We danced four songs before they shifted the beat. My Puerto Rican poontang was a good dancer and made sure she butted up against me on all sides of my body. She slathered on the charm and got two inches from my lips on more than one occasion. When I glanced to see if Mandy noticed—nothing. She was engrossed in the pool and the other girl.

The bullshit psycho-aerobics went on for two or three more hours before we decided to road trip it back to Charlottesville. Mandy drove me because I was too drunk and we followed Teeter and Kissie. We first had to stop at Wendy's so Kissie could get a burger. I tried to kiss Mandy in the drive-thru but she told me I was drunk and that I had to get sober before I tried to kiss her again. For a while, I just looked out the window and played like she didn't hurt my feelings.

Darkness enveloped I-64. There were no stars in the sky. There were no stars in my armored heart. The journeywork of the stars ended at the top of my crazy head where the channel to heaven and hell both began and ended. My brainal canal, the fjord, the ravine beneath the steep cliffs of sanity and insanity. Darfur and Puerto Rico and Canada. Why these places in my head all at once? I took out a penlight and read from the holy palm book. The first saint it talked about was Joan of Arc and how she saw the signs to her life fall from the sky and the voices in her head propelled her to become a glorious warrior for the French.

When we got back to my apartment, I took a happy, waggy Someday out back and drank my hundredth beer of the night. We both sat on the patio for a long while and I smoked three cigarettes while Teeter and Kissie stumbled to bed. Kissie made two bowls of Froot Loops, one for her and one for Teeter. I could hear her and Teeter laughing in the background saying radonkulous to describe just about everything.

Mandy silently drifted away.

"Piper! Are you going to bed?" Teeter yelled from down the hall. "Do you want some Froot Loops? I know you want some. Come on Pipsey, I know you want the loops."

"In a while," I yelled back. "Finish off the loops yourself, Radonkulita!"

"All right . . . don't stay up all night writing in some notebook and then talking some crazy philosophical delirious smack in the morning. It's going to be Sunday and you'll need to rest and we'll need to rest from your ramblings on how shit like the crack trade got started."

"Teeter, I don't know how the crack trade got started."

There was a pause and then I heard Kissie laughing. "It's good you don't know how the crack trade got started. Kissie thinks it's when boys trade girls each other's bootie around."

"Crack trade is good if you want a lot of action, then," I said.

"Good night. I won't be up late. Just till the morning light and then I'll read my womanifesto outside of your window till you get up. Or better yet sing you a song with my guitar."

"If you read your womanitfestival outside of my window, I'll make sure you never see crack again."

"Don't tell Mandy that," I laughed.

The apartment grew still.

"Well, Someday, it's you and me girl," I said to her and scratched her soft, rabbit-like ears. I rolled the palm of my hand down her smooth fur and held her paw. "I think we've come so far but I'm not sure where I'm supposed to go. Basketball feels somewhat right. I mean I'm okay but I don't know if it's what I want. Maybe we can just run away to Wyoming. Huh? What do you think girl? Run away to Wyoming and live on the range? I heard Jackson Hole is pretty. I could ride horses and you could follow me all day." Someday put her head on my thigh. Petting her for the next hour, I watched the darkness turn to morning light.

Before going to bed, I went out the front lawn and up the sharp slope and across the footbridge to Monroe Park. I drank one more beer and Someday lagged behind me sniffing bushes and peeing on everything. When we came back across the footbridge, Someday lay down on the grass and wouldn't move. Her hips hurt, I thought. So, I picked her up and carried her across the bridge. When we got back to the apartment, I carried her upstairs and deposited her at the foot of the bed.

When I crawled in bed, Mandy told me that I smelled like a brewery. Someday curled up at my feet and I turned my body completely around so my feet were on the pillow and my head was next to my dog's head. She licked me on the nose and I kissed her on hers.

"Someday is an excellent kisser. Aren't you girl?"

"I thought I was an excellent kisser?" Mandy whispered and shifted. "Close the door."

"I'm going to write the *Chronicles of Someday*. It will be part of my grand womanifesto—"

"Come up here, you dork. What's up with you? Have you been

up all night again? I don't see how you do it."

"Are you still mad at me?" I jumped out of bed.

"Yes. Boiling. You yell at me and then you go off and dance with some Latin girl for three hours."

"Oh, for crying out loud, Mandy. I danced a few songs with her. I didn't think you were watching, anyway." I slammed the door shut and jumped on the bed. I swaggered and then pulled my shirt up to show my stomach and did the backward bending belly, similar to downward facing dog but more fun.

"You should go back to see your grandfather."

"Why do you think people are so afraid?"

"Of what, goofy people like you?"

"I don't know. Have you ever been at the grocery store and were walking up and down the aisles and then everyone just averts his or her eyes from you after you make eye contact?"

"Piper. They see you coming and I'm surprised they don't run!" she yelled, then flung the pillow at me.

Teeter opened the door. Her shorts were hanging off her and her head was doing a 1970s throwback between Diana Ross and Michael Jackson.

I screamed, "Jesus, Teeter, what happened to your wig?"

"Leave my wig out of this. You all have to be quiet in here. I can hear everything you're saying. Did you see the throw up in the den? I think your dog got sick. You better clean it up before I step on it and then California's gonna have to invent a new Richter scale to register it."

Then from down the hallway, Kissie throated out the loudest bid. "If you all be quiet then I'll buy brunch. It's Sunday, ya'll shut the hell up. Teeter if you start working on that wig of yours now, it'll be just good enough to be able to cover it with a baseball cap."

"I'm going to kick her ass. Now, you two start kissing or something so we can sleep."

Aligning my body over top of Mandy's, I threw a sock sideways behind me at the door as Teeter walked out. "Do I have to flirt with you to get you to kiss me?"

Mandy reached up and grabbed the back of my head and mashed her lips into mine. My whole head buzzed when our hips, like chips of flint, rubbed and moved in circular rhythm—spontaneously she moved to the right of my under folds and thrust up and around. I pushed down and back following her sexy, circular line together. Then again and again and again while our mouths stayed hovering in the hot, breathy air between us. With our lips parted and the temperature two hundred degrees between our legs, she softly forced her tongue into my mouth and then went farther in than I wanted, but I let it come in. Three times, she pulled her tongue out then in—each time faster till I grabbed the tuft of hair on the back of her neck and forced her mouth and tongue into me as far as I could take. Simultaneously, we both murmured a sweet issue of love. No words. Just a murmur. She moaned, pulled away, looked at me and smiled, then did it again till I thought my face and head would melt. Then she put her muscular forearms onto the curves of my lower back and reached for the edge of my denim shirt and pulled it over my head.

"Are you pissed off at me?" I asked more breathy than before.

"Yes."

I leaned down, the sinews in my skinny arms bulging wide, the blood running fast. "Say it again, Mandy."

"What?"

"Yes. Say yes. Say it!" My voice and mouth were strong in her ear.

She waited a moment and I pulled away to see her eyes wide and open then she said in a mouthy whisper, "Yes. Yes. Yes."

"Do you believe me when I say the things I do?" I kissed her.

"Yes." She pulled back and whispered again.

I put my tongue in her mouth and pulled away. "Do you see what I see . . . come on. Do you see it?"

"Yes," she responded and closed her eyes.

She grabbed me from behind and our whole frontal vortices between our head and torso and hips were rotating and rising and falling and pulling and pushing in one convoluted sex mélange. The fluidity of the slow motioning gave way to the tension of the stroking, finding, licking, kissing and flicking of our tongues. We became bodies annealing to the skin of each other and I was giddy in my head and she was giddy in hers.

"I want you deep inside me," Mandy said from a scratchy throat.

"Say it. Say it again," I whispered as her sweaty hair became enmeshed in my sweaty face. We were face to face.

I pulled my hips away from hers. Then I slowly came down on her and seared into her vagina with the side of my thigh and rubbed hard against her hollow hips. Three times I did this and then I stopped and asked her in her ear, "Do you feel that?"

"Yes."

Under her waist I drew my index and middle fingers down and slithered them in and around the lace to the undercoat of wetness that was sliding down from the soft folds of the inward fleshy opening and onto the sheets. A mixture of viscous sweat and oil and flesh. Moaning. She was moaning. *Come on Piper,* I thought I heard her say.

"Are you still mad at me?" I asked.

"Yes."

"Do you want me?"

"Yes."

"Then feel me, Mandy. Feel me." I found the opening to her vagina. The long vessel my fingers longed to plunge into and to feel the tip of her fleshy cervix. My index finger and middle finger coupled together slid all the way in and up on the first entry . . . I went all the way there—to her cervix—she moaned and I moaned.

"You like that?"

"Yes."

I did it again. Thrusting in her with both fingers and whispering in her ear, "I want you. Do you feel me wanting you?"

"Yes. Don't stop—"

I kissed her slow and deep and hard while keeping inside of her and then pulled away. "No fucking way." I wanted her and felt mad inside my own body and head for her. I was boiling hot and sweating and going in circles with my legs and hips . . . faster and then slowly and then stopping without warning to penetrate her with my thick strong fingers. There was an intense lathering of excitement between my legs I'd never felt before.

She arched her back slowly. I told her to flip over and then put my wet fingers into her from behind. I placed my left hand on her shoulder and pulled her into my fingers as I was going in and out and out and in from behind. Then suddenly, she told me to stop.

"Why? Are you okay?" I giggled and smiled and kissed her neck. Mandy was quiet.

I kissed her fully and then on the bridge of her neck and down to her heart. Pulling and stroking her delicate skin between my lips and teeth, she made soft tones of pleasure and I increased my pressure with more of what I felt she wanted. I softly kissed the soulful belly and the ridge of her pubic hair that was dense and dark and shaved in the folds of her legs. For a second, I thought I saw a small spider crawl across the top of her thigh, but I wafted it away into the essence of the air. It floated away on imaginary filament.

The bridge of rapture.

Then I heard Someday moan and then cry out beside the bed. Stopping, I put my lips on the inside of Mandy's thighs and then heard Someday begin the *whirfulling* belching dogs do before getting sick.

"What's wrong girl?" I put my hand on her convulsing back. Then the blood came out of her mouth.

"Jesus Christ. It's bloody," I said and leaned over the edge.

"I'm bloody?" Mandy put her hands in between her legs.

"No. Someday's got blood everywhere." Then I saw a trail of blood under the bed. "Get up!" Mandy didn't move. "Get up. Mandy, Get up!"

"Okay. Geez. You don't have to yell!"

Suddenly, I was buzzing from head to toe. My body became electric circuits and fiery bolts of energy surged through my body. Someday lowered her head and attempted to lick up her vomit—I told her no and pulled her away with her collar. Hopping on the floor, I grabbed part of the sheet and wiped her mouth with it. She licked my face and I stroked her head again. Her nose was hot and dry.

My beer buzz was still in me, but the adrenaline had my head clanging.

Panic.

"Teeter! Teeter! Get the car started," I yelled down the hallway. "Someday's throwing up blood . . . hurry!" I pulled on my jeans and shirt and lay down on the floor. She was panting and licking me all at the same time. "Hurry!"

Mandy dressed and ran down the hallway. "I'll get a towel . . . and a blanket."

Kissie came into the room and just stared at the blood. Mandy bounded back and Teeter yelled from downstairs that we needed gas.

Wrapping the fleece blanket around her, I picked her up and she lost control of her bowels. There was blood and stool all over her and me and the ground.

I kissed her on her soft muzzle. "Hold on. Hold on. Hold on. Hold on, girl. You're my good girl. I know. I can feel it when you kiss—I can feel it when you kiss me." She moaned when I shifted. It came out long and slow and guttural.

"She's really sick, Mandy. She was moping around the last couple of days. But, Kissie, did you notice anything different?"

"Naw. I like Someday but I'm scared of dogs, mainly. I can barely touch 'em. My uncle nearly got his ass chewed off by a dog one time . . . and—"

"Spare the story right now, Kissie. Come on, Piper. Let's get her in the car." Mandy looked worried. Her eyes were tight and pinched.

Then I was Alice in Wonderland. The surreal moment enlarged itself on the walls of the hallway and everything tunneled in my vision.

Delicately balancing myself at the top of the steps, I crept down the flight finding each step with my leather shoe. The walls came in and made it tight. My hands squeezed tightly around Someday's fur. I held her good front leg and her back legs with all my strength.

Unwieldy and delicate, we both made it through the front door that Kissie held open. She reached out and touched Someday's deformed paw. We made eye contact briefly. Her eyes were like pinballs and they turned to crosses.

When I got to my truck, I gently placed my now listless dog in the back stretch of the club cab. I told Mandy and Teeter to get in.

Teeter stopped dead in her tracks. "That's all right, I'm scared of hospitals even if they're vet hospitals." I flashed my eyes at her. "But, today seems like a good day to face those fears." Her arms akimbo, she looked at Mandy.

Holy mother of God, I thought. What is going on?

Mandy stood by the side of the door. "Is she dead?"

"No. But all that blood is not good." I leaned over to the backseat and petted her head. "Come on girl. You're all right." I felt her shallow breathing. Her eyes opened for a second and then closed again.

Teeter climbed in the front seat. "What do you think is wrong? What happened?"

"She's bleeding. We need to get her to the emergency vet right away—"

Pulling my cell phone from my pocket, I hiccupped and then looked to the road. Four male BRU students in sunglasses came down the hill in their Saturday night clothes. Each had coffee in his hand.

Panic.

"Call the emergency vet. Now! Now! Now—" I yelled toward Teeter and watched the four students as I fumbled to put the keys in the ignition. The arms of one of the students turned to boa constrictor snakes and then I was way out of control. Mandy stood by the truck window. I yelled, "Get in the truck, Mandy!"

"Stop yelling. You'll scare the shit out of your dog!" Teeter was dialing on my phone.

"She's already pooped all over everything and me. Mandy, either get the fuck in the truck or out of my way! Teeter, can you help me? Mandy are you coming?"

Mandy did not respond.

"What's wrong with you Mandy? Huh. Why don't you go back inside and masturbate then." I peeled away with Someday in the backseat of the car.

Once we got on the main Route 29, I drove over 120 miles per hour to the emergency vet on the outskirts of Charlottesville. Teeter kept putting her arm on my shoulder and then kept yelling, "Slow the hell down. Piper easy. Slow down . . . you might kill us all before we even get there!"

But, I did not hear her. I refused to hear her.

All I could see was Someday as a puppy, her dark damp slick body limping along the James River to find me and my brother Jack there by the side of the mossy bank. She must have spotted me and Jack and my parents long before we ever saw her. Slipping down to the marshy shore from the end of the old bridge and tentative and uncertain of her small body and three legs, she clumsily ambled across the tiny bridge to find us. It must have been quite the journey for her in her shepherd's body. She must have smelled the bait on dad's fishing line, she must have nosed the grass and air to smell the perfume that emanated from my mother's body. She must have heard the playful laughter of children on some strange day of her new existence. She had lost her mother, too, and perhaps her siblings. We never knew if she'd been left there or where her first home or family was.

All of us walked across the old bridge that day, with Someday in my arms, to the thicket of trees on the other side but we found no signs of other dogs or a mother. Jack held her on her return trip back. We concluded that Someday, not even close to six weeks old, came to us all by herself; that she was compelled to find me and Jack and once with us, she knew she'd found a home. We were judge and jury on that one. My mom and dad both said that our dog had found us. Dad said that sometimes the best things in life come our way when we least expect them, same went for the worst things in life.

Just a few years later, I saw my brother getting into a pickup truck with my mom and dad and remember my mom telling me to stay back because Someday was sick. They wouldn't be long at the hospital. They wouldn't be long. They wouldn't be long. They wouldn't be long. Long. Long. Long.

Panic. Fuck.

Teeter helped me get my dying dog out of the truck. She was dying, I knew, because my heart was breaking. The back of my heart had a pin prick and it had been slowly leaking since my special dog came in and saved my life; leaking because my spirit knew this would one day come. Like a longing you never knew existed. It was there. Very there. I whispered sweet somethings and sang a made-up song to her like I did on most days. *Someday you are my girl. Someday is my dog. Someday when you kiss me, I pine away. Someday, someday you are my love. Someday, someday way up above. Someday, someday . . ."*

They took her into the back of the vet hospital and told us to wait. Teeter got a magazine and I paced around the front lobby looking at dog food, worried people and the girl who checked people in behind the counter. She was befuddled most of the time and exasperated at how long it took people to get their stories straight as to what happened and did they have the money to pay for it.

I called Vera and Andrea and Jenny and left a message. It was Sunday. They were surely down at the MCC church in Banff and then they would go to lunch. I might not get them for a while.

Teeter got up. "You want some coffee?"

"Sure," I exhaled.

"Okay. Be right back. Save my spot. You okay?"

"Yeah."

Then she hugged me. "You know you made me come down here and my wig is all messed up. What if I meet the man of my dreams at the coffee shop next door and he sees my wig like this? I'm blaming you and that dog of yours."

"Teeter, if you weren't straight, I'd kiss you."

"Shoo. You can kiss me. Just no tongue, then you'll really get my wig all messed up."

I slapped her on the butt.

"You want me to call Coach DuPont or Coach Potter and let them know something is up?" she asked.

"No. Let's wait till we see what they say."

As Teeter walked out, a handsome, clean-cut black guy in an army uniform walked in with his kitten and checked in with the girl at the front. When she asked him if he had the money to pay for treatment, he said he didn't care how much it cost and that he had just jumped from an airplane and had found this kitten in the field where he landed.

"Must have been some jump," I said as he sat down next to me. "What's your kitten's name?"

"I think I'm going to name her Leon. I just jumped from a plane carrying an old dead paratrooper named Leon to Westhampton Cemetery. When I landed—it was quite the landing—this kitty was in the field next to the graveyard. Her front paw is torn up some. I may have gotten her with a line from my chute. She was a tangled mess. It took me an hour to free her from my parachute. I think she needs stitches."

"I'm a little confused. You just jumped out of a plane with a dead man?"

"Yep. It's a little well-known secret among us paratroopers. Especially ones who fought in any war. We love jumping out of planes and when any one of us dies, we go back up in a plane and give them one last jump before putting them in the ground."

I looked at the kitten's paw. "I've never heard of such a thing."

"She's cute, isn't she? Yeah. It's a tribute for them and their lives and for their families. It kind of brings things full circle."

"That's remarkable."

"I'm Jay Kennedy." He extended his hand.

"Piper Cliff." We shook hands.

"So, Piper, got an animal here?"

"Yeah. My dog. She's in there. Pretty sick."

"Oh, I'm sorry. How long has she been in there?"

"Just a little while . . . she's twelve years old."

"Can you hold her for a second?" He handed over the kitten before I could respond. I held her paw and stroked her ears. Snuggling against me, she closed her eyes.

"Hey, Leon, you're a cutie. Looks like Daddy is going to get you fixed up!"

He pulled out his wallet and showed me a picture of his wife and son and their dog. "That's Harper, our yellow Lab. My wife and son are crazy about her. Isn't she cute?"

"Yes. She sure is."

"What's your occupation, Piper?"

I thought on this for a second. "I'm a writer."

"Oh, a writer. What do you write?"

"Well, nothing really yet. But I've got a lot of ideas I'm scrawling down. Good ones. I think they are worth listening to."

"Well, I'm sure you have some great ideas . . . are you published?"

"Not yet. But I'm dreaming about it. You know the old adage. When you've got a dream, you've got to grab it and never let go."

"Who said that?"

"I don't know. My mom used to say it to me."

"Well, your mom sounds like a very smart woman."

"She is. She's a very smart woman. Really pretty, too."

The girl from behind the counter stood up. "Mr. Kennedy. The doctor can see you in room four now. Ms. Cliff, the doctor wants to see you in room one in about five minutes. You can go on in." My stomach dropped and I nodded my head.

"Good luck with Leon," I said.

"You, too, with your dog. Tell your mom to keep giving you those good inspirations." He took Leon from my grasp and walked down the foyer to the examining room.

Teeter walked in and handed me the coffee. "What's his name?"

"Who?"

"That good-looking man with the kitty, you know who."

"Oh! That was Jay Kennedy."

"Well he's cute and black and he's got on a uniform. Did you get any info on him, girl?"

"The doctor is coming to see us about Someday in room one. Get your butt in there. Did you bring any sugar?"

"Oh, honey, I'm all the sugar you need!"

"Shut up and get in there before I kick your butt." She had made me laugh. Something I didn't think I could do under the circumstances.

Chapter 9

We waited for an hour of eternity as I wore small trenches pacing around Teeter and the examining table, till the doctor finally came in. We went through the ordinary pleasantries and I watched him pause three or four times before he got his words together. Teeter looked back and forth between him and me trying to figure out the gravity of it all.

"She's got hemorrhagic gastroenteritis," the doctor finally told me as I stood with my arms crossed. "We're not sure why it happens, but it is seen in breeds of Someday's kind."

He placed the clipboard on the metal counter. Teeter sat in the chair in the corner.

"What can we do?" I asked.

Silence.

Then, "Well. I'm sorry . . ." He hesitated. "We're going to have to make some tough decisions today. Your dog is bleeding internally and her heart is enlarged."

Teeter exhaled loudly and said, "Oh, Lord, girl."

"Is she comfortable back there? Can we see her?" I asked, then looked at the door like it might open and she would bound through.

"This is going to be painful, Ms. Cliff. But your dog is probably not going to make it through this. We are at a big crossroads—" The doctor stopped and glanced at Teeter.

"Can you operate?" Teeter asked.

"No. She's too compromised. Her liver count is off the chart and from what we can gather from the ultrasound, her stomach is twisted."

"How much pain is she in?" I asked. "Pain, pain . . ." I covered my mouth. "I don't want my dog in any pain, pain." I put my hands on my lips and twisted them to stop. "Do you understand?"

"Yes. We've sedated her and given her some fluids but she's a bit anxious. I know this is a hard decision. But, there's not much we can do for your dog, ma'am. I'm very sorry."

"Can I see her? She doesn't like places like this, you know."

"Yes, I'll get Eddie to bring her in. Wait here. It'll be a few minutes."

Teeter stood up. "If we wait any longer, a new wing is going to be built in my name."

I took off my denim shirt and tucked my T-shirt in. "Put her here on my shirt. Help me make sure they do that, okay? Not on this table. Down here on my shirt . . . Teeter—"

"Yeah, hon . . ."

"Will you come here and stand next to me? Will you hold my hand?"

Teeter stood next to me and put one hand on my shoulder and then interlocked her other hand in mine. "Okay. Okay . . . this is the right thing to do, you know. She's been your good girl. Oh, Jesus. Come on Jesus. We need you now Jesus. Come on Mom and Dad we need Jesus!"

They brought the dog in who had saved my life so many years ago and gently laid her on my denim shirt in the corner of the examining room. I laid down on the floor next to her. "Just give me a few minutes with her and then we can put her down. Okay, okay, okay . . . I need to talk to her." The doctor and the technician left and Teeter sat in the chair behind me, putting her hand on my back.

Where was God for my breaking spirit? I needed Him now more than ever. Please God. Please God. Please help her . . .

Someday was breathing heavily and her eyes were half open and red. I stroked her from her head to her tail and gazed into her eyes. She looked into mine. We regarded and admired each other like dog and guardian do. I closed my eyes and she closed hers—opening once again to meet in the bridge of light between us.

"In my mind's eye, Teeter . . ." I blubbered. "There are no words to describe, not one vowel, not one syllable, not even a great line of poetry or prose to flesh out my love for this dog." I fingered her collar and her tag and scratched the skin of her neck where she liked it. We locked our eyes, our hearts, our souls and our devoted love in these final moments of her precious life. The dog who was born to save me and I who was born to save her. She was my forever dog—my forever girl. "Nothing, you hear me girl." I pushed my head into her neck and into her fur and stroked her ears. "Nothing will ever take you and me away. You have been my everyday, my everyway, my anyway, my always . . . you hear, me. I love you more than anything. More than anything. You hear me. Teeter?"

"Yeah, hon?" She stroked my back.

"I'm with her to the very end, aren't I?"

"Yes, you are."

"It wasn't that way with Mom and Dad and Jack. I wasn't with them. I wasn't with them. I wasn't with them . . ." I couldn't stop the words.

"Hang on baby girl. Hang on—" Teeter wrapped her arms around me—"Let her go and find them, girl. Let her go and find them. They're waiting for her. They on that bridge you told me about waiting for her . . . same bridge where she found you all so long ago honey . . . that's where she came from and that's where she going back. Your mom is there. Your dad is there. Jack is there. Jack wants his time with her now Piper. Let her go to him and your family. It's her home, Piper. Let her go home."

"Call the doctor then. Bring them in," I said.

I held my angel dog in my arms while they put the plastic tubing around her good paw and inserted the needle, then the fluid that would stop her heart. For a second, mine stopped, too.

"Bless you, my dog. Bless you . . . bless you," I repeated the words like a church bell might clang over and over and over till I passed out from the insurmountable grief that infused itself all over me and pulled me to the ground black, weighty and sludge-like.

Teeter put her arms around me and we rocked there for a long while. Someday was gone. But I felt her spirit in the room there with us—the spirit that had brought her from the bridge that day, the spirit that had stayed with me for twelve years, the spirit of her that would stay with me forever. Her spirit was breaking through. Chills raced up and down my body.

The doctor and technician left us there alone.

"She was a good dog," Teeter said finally. "I never seen a dog who loved anyone like she loved you. You could see it in the way she limped around you all the time and looked at you. Even followed you in the bathroom for crying out loud."

I smiled. "I know. We barely spent any time apart. She was always with me. Even when I went somewhere in the truck. She always went with me, you know. Always."

The woman from the front desk came back in and asked for a credit card and Teeter told her to get the hell out.

The technician came in and shaved a piece of fur off for me and put it into a special box. Then I took her collar off and kissed her for a long while. I wrapped her in my denim shirt and told them to take care of her body.

We stayed for another hour and then Teeter paid for it. I never saw the bill.

We drove back to the apartment in silence while I fingered Someday's collar in my front pocket.

• • •

I didn't make it to most of my classes the week after Someday died. Instead, I found myself driving around town and reading *Palms of the Holy* at any local bar I happened into. Vera, Jenny and Andrea had called me twice a day at least to check on me but I told them I didn't want to talk about it. With Someday gone, I had lost all hope. Everything I had had up until then was all about the two of us together. Now, I felt like one act instead of two. The life we had led together for over twelve years had ended and I was paralyzed. Mandy had not talked to me since she died. I guessed she was a weak asshole who couldn't write English compositions. Fuck her, I thought. Fuck everyone.

Even though I wanted to quit BRU basketball and become a drug addict and alcoholic, I went to practice anyway. Benumbed through most of the drills, I heard Coach Potter in the distance directing the team to do this offense, then switch to this defense, and I roboticized myself through it all. She didn't say much to me the first two weeks after my dog died but then one afternoon she pulled me aside.

"Come in, Piper." She waved me into her office. She was typing on her laptop but stopped and then closed the cover halfway down. "Sit down. You want some water or something?" Her office had diplomas on the wall and two retired numbers in wooden frames from two of her NCAA Kodak players of the year: 1988 and 1992. It was a small office but neatly organized with a flat screen TV in the corner and a leather sofa behind an oak coffee table. Coach Potter was wearing a BRU T-shirt and matching sweats. Game DVDs littered her desk along with three clipboards and two whistles. It was the first time I'd been in to have a chat.

"No, ma'am," I said. "I'm okay."

"Well. I know you're okay. You're one of the best freshman pure shooters I've ever recruited. Carla!" she yelled into the adjacent office, "will you bring in a couple of waters for me and Piper here." She paused and looked at me. "I'm sorry about you losing your dog, Piper. I lost my little Snowy about a year ago. Losing a dog is like losing your best friend, I know. I've been there. I talked to your folks in Canada earlier today."

"You did?" This declaration made me feel odd. I wanted a beer if this conversation was going to persist.

Carla brought in the two waters and handed one each to us.

Coach Potter opened hers and drank it like a beer, guzzling the first three or for sips into one long one. She belched.

"Yes. I did. I talked to Andrea. She's your foster parent, right?"

"Yes. Andrea and Jenny are my foster parents and Vera is one of my guardians."

"She seemed nice enough. I told them that I was worried about you."

"Why?"

"Well, since you lost your dog, you've been going through the motions at practice like you're not even here. Then, come to find out, your history and English teachers say you haven't turned in three of your last four assignments. Now, I know losing a dog is hard, but you need to buck up a little bit and get your act together. Oneday was a good companion for you. But I know that Teeter is a good room-mate. Why don't you get her to help you with some of your work till you get caught up. Coach DuPont could help, too."

"Yeah, Piper, I could help." I turned around to see him leaning in the doorway. Wearing a pair of jeans and sweatshirt, he looked like he was garnished by a whistle and a baseball cap.

"Her name was Someday," I corrected my coach.

She took another sip of her water and put her feet up on the chair in front of her. "Someday—funny name for a dog. I like Oneday. Like one day I'm going to get my act together in spite of losing some-one close." She looked at Coach Dupont.

He sat in the chair next to me. "Mandy Weaver told us about your not going to some classes, Piper. She also said that she was worried about your drinking. You know you can get into big trouble being underage and all."

"Everyone on the team drinks," I said.

"Not everyone and not every day," he said.

Coach Potter stood up. "Mandy also said that you spend a lot of time driving around town and going up in the mountains by yourself. Is that true?"

"What's wrong with that?"

"Nothing," Coach Dupont said, "but if you're driving around half the day, you obviously are not studying. Look, we're not here to berate you or to get information from you. We just want you to get better so that you can be happy both on and off the court. Okay?"

"Okay. Is that all?" I felt like Coach Potter was a tad pissy.

"No. After I talked to Andrea, I asked if they might want to come for a visit. She said they were already planning on one. I also found out that she's bringing her partner. What's her name?"

"Jenny."

"Yes, Jenny. This is your other mother?"

"My mother is dead."

"Where's your father?"

"Dead. And, I'm fucking dead without my dog. Dead. Dead. Dead." I got up and walked out and spat on the hallway floor. They called after me and came into the hallway. I heard Coach DuPont tell Coach Potter, "Let her be."

Driving back to my apartment, I decided to stop off at La Taza and have a margarita and get a burger to go. Three cigarettes and two margaritas later, I opened one of my spiral notebooks and began to write, scrawl and doodle. I watched a man and a woman making goo-goo eyes at each other at a small table next to mine and there were six BRU students laughing and cackling over themselves to beat the bar band in the corner booth. They were handsome. Three guys and three girls. One guy had short blond hair and a T-shirt that said 333 Only Half-Devilish. Internally giggling, I licked the salt off my drink and swallowed the alcohol till I could feel it begin to slow my blood but boil my thoughts. Alcohol was good. Very good. I loved it.

Between the margaritas and the beer, I felt as if my intelligence increased itself. And the more I drank, the smarter I became and the musings in my notebook were off-the-hook philosophy. I mastered quantum physics in a single bound. I verified that Jesus Christ had lived and that his bloodline had started somewhere off the coast of Africa and ended up with the Mormons in this latter day for the whole world to see on the one hand and then not see on the other. I drew a map of the United States and put a big circular spiral on Idaho. Evidently Idaho is in heaven, which means that, in fact, heaven is on earth. I traced all good writing from the beginning of time to now to the book *The Color Purple* by Alice Walker. She understood what spirits were and had put them all together in a book that won the Pulitzer prize. She didn't know when she was writing it that the book would change the world. But when it was done, the spiral effect (of which I noted when I drew the boot of Texas) would help millions of people understand the effects of love and triumph. Good writing, Alice. I wrote this in my notebook. I also wrote that Shakepeare was right. I also wrote that William Blake needed to learn more about the plight of fleas. Not sure what I meant by that but sometimes when you're smart, really smart, you're not sure what you're aiming for or what the hell you're talking about.

When I looked up from my scribblings, Mandy Weaver was walking in the door with Coach Potter. My soul did a flip up and down. Then I put my pen down and slid under the table. I pulled my phone from my pocket and texted Teeter.

Get uR ass down to La Taza. Under the table in the corner. Can't get out. You'll understand later. P.

I waited a moment or two. Then hers came back.

Will b there in ten minutes. Order me some food. Will be in doo-rag and

slippers. T.

I texted her back.

Okay. Will double my order. Mandy is with Potter. Don't let on I'm here. P.

Then hers.

You're dumb.

Teeter had not read my philosophies. Cowering there, I reached to the table and pulled out a cigarette and lit it. The waitress came by and glanced under the table and asked if everything was all right. I told her that I was avoiding my boyfriend and please double my burger order and then I'd pay and get out. She signaled that she understood by handing me an ashtray. If Potter knew I was smoking in a bar, she'd kick me off the team. Now she was sitting with my girlfriend at a nearby table and she could kiss my smart ass.

After two cigarettes, Teeter sat down at the table. She had bunny slippers on and sweats and a pink sweatshirt.

"How did you find me?" I asked.

"Smoke signals, dumb radonkulous ass," she laughed. "Did you order me some food?"

"Yes. Do you see Potter and Weaver? What are they doing?"

"They are way over on the other side. It's hard to tell. Potter has a glass of wine and Weaver has a beer and . . ."

"I don't care what they're drinking. Why do you think they are together?"

"Oh, Piper. You didn't know about last year? Mandy didn't tell you?"

"Tell me what, Teeter?"

"There were big rumors that her and Coach Potter were an item. Very hush-hush. Then at the end of the season, Mandy got so depressed that none of us knew what to do for her. I figured it out though. I think Potter dropped her because she was afraid someone would find out she was a-baking the clam with her."

"Baking clams. You're sick, Teeter."

"That's me and I'm not the one who's gay. Piper?"

"Yeah?"

"What's all this shit you've written in this notebook here?"

"Oh, shit. Just give it to me. Hand it here. Don't read it, Teeter. I'm embarrassed."

"You think heaven is in Idaho? Piper, have you lost your mind? Heaven isn't in Idaho."

"Where is it then? Hand me a cigarette."

"Heaven is just twenty-six miles down the road. My parents' house."

"Teeter that's the gayest thing I've ever heard."

"Well, if Shakespeare is right then I guess I might have something to say, too."

"I haven't even been to your parents' house."

"You can't come. Piper, I think people are starting to look at me funny with you under the table and all. I think if you sit up and get next to me that Potter and Weaver aren't going to see you. I can barely see them."

I sat up, lit a cigarette, and guzzled the rest of my drink. Teeter blocked my view.

"I'm worried about you, roommate," Teeter said, finally.

I put my drink down. "Why?"

"Well, you have too many freckles, for one. And, you've been drinking like a maniac since your dog died. I don't mind you drinking, Piper. Hell, I like to drink, too. But, you're not sleeping. I hear you get up and go out on the porch at night to smoke and fiddle with that guitar of yours. You talk sometimes like you're nuts."

"That's the spirit, Teeter. Way to get me cheered up. I was hoping for a burger and some conversation like, 'I can't believe your girlfriend is out with her ex-love the basketball coach.' But no, you're more worried about a few extra drinks since the love of my life died."

"Okay. Sorry. Still like me?"

"Yes. So, why can't I go see your folks?"

"I was just kidding with you. You can. Anytime you want."

"Why do you think Mandy's out with Potter?"

"I don't know. Since Someday died, she's been kind of scarce. I know she's worried about you, too. Maybe she's out talking to her about you?"

"No. She was weird before Someday died. I fought with her after seeing my grandfather in Richmond and things have been tense ever since. Oh, well."

"How's he doing?"

"I don't know. The old fart is on his deathbed, I think. Andrea and Jenny are coming to see me week after next."

"Good. I'll make myself scarce on Sunday. I'll go see my folks."

"You can stay."

"Nah. I'll hang out Saturday, but then I need to see them."

The waitress brought over Teeter's order of food. Then as we walked out the door, I stole a look Mandy's way. Directly—she was looking directly into Coach Potter's eyes. That's the spirit, I thought. Your girlfriend's dog dies and you're back fucking the coach.

Chapter 10

"I'm not fucking Coach Potter! For Christ's sake, Piper, she's almost twenty years older than me!" Mandy slammed her hand down on the kitchen counter. The beer caps, all fourteen from the night before that littered the counter, jumped up in syncopation.

I turned to the fridge and retrieved a beer. I got one for her.

"Well, when I saw you at La Taza last night it looked like you were staring into her eyes like she was something more than your coach. You said you were studying and that you would talk to me later. You never called, Mandy. Where were you?"

"I went home. Nothing happened. You can believe what you want but nothing happened! This is bullshit, anyway. What's wrong with you? Your dog is dead. I know that but you need to get your shit together. You're off driving up in the mountains and you spend more time scribbling in your notebooks than going to class. What are you writing down? What's so important?"

"Nothing. Nothing is important, Mandy. Just go."

"Are you writing some sort of manuscript or something? You've got notebooks full of stuff you never share."

"You're right. It's nothing."

"Well it must be some important nothing, then. I don't know Piper. You're a funny character. I like you and have fun with you. But—"

I filled the words in. "Maybe it's time to spend more time apart because it's really you and not me and you just need time to figure it all out. I've had the speech before, Weaver. You're not the first."

She swallowed a swig then put her hands on her hips. Her phone rang but she ignored it. "Why don't we start over in a week or two. Just give me two weeks away and then we can start fresh. I just need to think without you blabbering about all of your ideas about creation and women's suffrage and whatever art fucking movement is moving you at the time. Okay?"

"Is that Coach Potter calling you? You need to go in early for practice? Or does she want you to stay late?"

"There isn't practice today. Remember?"

Teeter walked in wearing the same doo rag that she had the night before. She eyed me all the way to the fridge and retrieved a Sprite. "Hey, you two. Weaver, how's it going?"

"Good, Teeter."

"Piper, you?"

"I'm fine, Teeter."

There was a pause for a second and then she said, "Well, that's the spirit. Go ahead and ask how ole Teeter is. How she ain't had no dick in six months and she thinking about going to the Lesbo a-go-go to maybe find some pussy? Huh? What you two think about that?"

"Call Theonia. She needs some big pussy to contend with," I said.

"You two are something," Mandy put her beer down. "I'm leaving this den of iniquity and going home."

"You don't even know what iniquity is."

"Fuck you, Piper." Then she walked out the front door with a slam.

Teeter sat on the barstool by the counter and retied her rag. "You okay?"

I shrugged.

"She fucking Coach Potter."

"She says she isn't. Want to go to Richmond with me today?"

"Hell no. Today is pedicure and manicure day. Kara and Kissie are coming over and so is Jessie. You want yours done?"

"No thanks. I am going to wallow in my own misery. I've lost Someday and now my hot girlfriend. Perhaps I'll celebrate by driving to California and finding Hilary Swank to make out with."

"She's straight. She's not going to fool with you, you freak show note writer. You better off writing up some sex scene in one of your notebooks and just re-reading it a bunch of times to get it in your head. Otherwise, it ain't happening. You might want a pedicure, though, if you're going to make the drive."

"Yeah, perhaps a pedicure."

"Saneha is coming over, too."

"Talk about someone who's crazier than me. I can't believe Potter hasn't kicked her off the team yet." I swallowed and then sat down next to Teeter.

Teeter got a toothpick and picked at her teeth. "She won't get rid of her. She's too good. Plus she's on a full ride. I think if she kicks her off, then she loses dat big ole scholarship money. She can't give it to anyone else."

"Oh. My parents are going to croak when they see my semester grades. They'll single-handedly remove me from the team before I flunk out of school. You want a beer?" I asked.

Teeter looked at her watch and rolled her eyes then got up and made a bowl of Froot Loops. "Coach Potter will talk with you first. She's worried you won't be ready for the tournament coming up. It's a big one and you've been going through the motions in practice."

"She did talk to me."

"When?"

"Yesterday. She was talking about losing my dog but getting my act together. Problem is. I don't know what act I'm in. Is it act one of my life? The new beginning. Is it act two of my life? Lose your girlfriend and the missing college year? Is it act three of my life . . . ?"

"How about just get your act together, girl? Let that be your new act."

"Come and go to Richmond with me, Teet. I promise I won't take you to the old fort like last time. We'll just stop in and see the old man and go to Shockoe Sally's and dance the night away."

"Go ahead. Why don't you call Natalie Wingfield? She's a gaybird and might want to go."

"You think?"

"She's not a big talker though. She doesn't drink much either."

"We'll fix that. What's her number? You got her programmed?"

Teeter handed me her phone and I scrolled through the address book. Glancing down to the floor, I noticed Someday's dog bowls still lying where they always did. I looked away.

"Wingfield? It's Piper. Yeah," I looked at Teeter and covered the phone. "Her voice is mousy."

"She can probably hear you, dumbass." Teeter rolled her eyes and moved herself and her cereal to the couch.

"I'm doing a road trip to Richmond to go dancing. You want to go? Oh, come on. It'll be fun. We'll go see my dying grandfather after we go to my old homestead and then I pay your way into the bar. What do you think? The girls in Richmond will never be the same? Uh-huh? Oh, Weaver. She's got a date with some older chick and can't go. Break up? No. Taking a break. Whatever that means. Look Wingfield. I'm not asking you on a date or anything. I just want some company to Richmond. It's only an hour and I'll talk your head off, I promise. Super. Come to my place around six o'clock. We'll be in Richmond by seven and out dancing by nine thirty. You can be back here passed out on the couch by two in the morning. Okay, you're right. I'll be passed out on the couch by two in the morning." I shut the phone.

Teeter slurped the remnants of her cereal. "I can't believe she's going with you."

"That's the spirit, Teet. Way to believe in your roomie. Hey, are those good?"

"Froot Loops? Have a bowl, girl. It'll take you right to Idaho. Where you think heaven is. I swear I've never met anyone as dumb as you."

"Teeter. You are GAY! I know you want me. Come on let's go upstairs and get the straight out of you. It'll be you and me in the first sex scene of my womanifesto."

"Piper, you're going to be in Idaho soon if you don't clamp it. And if I'm going to be in your womanifesto, it better be with Jamie Foxx and I'm on top. You hear?"

"Got it. This is good cereal. It makes fruity milk."

"Shut your dumbster and hand me the clicker, fruitania. Judge Judy is about to come on."

The pull to go to Richmond was like a calling, a weird tolling, perhaps—especially since Someday died. The footbridge lay there with its overgrown grass and the pier where we used to fish. It saw no visitors but bore its days out in the serene melancholy of its lone river watch. The shallow shore still held the skipped rocks my brother and mother threw years before. They lay deep in the silty water but were there in the memory of themselves and the memory of me.

I would die on this trip to Richmond to see my grandfather.

It was about time I did.

The signs had been there since I left Canada to come home.

The cure for paralysis was coming through me on the wings of Joan of Arc. I can tell you this now. Joan of Arc is hot. She's one hot saint.

The angels had been on my shoulders since Someday broke through and I was starting to listen to what they were whispering in my ear. Mainly, they were making me stop at any old place and go to the bathroom. Hitting four roadside gas stations on the way to Richmond, Natalie Wingfield asked me if I needed to buy some Depends and pee in them. I told her to shut up.

At exit 154, I looked in my rearview mirror and saw Houdini sitting in the backseat fettered to the side door. He winked at me. Then I winked back. He told me in his head to turn the radio station and that a certain song would give me a message. Flipping the buttons, I became confused because my phone rang. Natalie took over the radio. My stomach dropped when I looked back to see that Houdini was morphing into something else. Slightly nervous, I flipped the phone open.

It was Vera.

"Hey, Vera. What's up?" The connection was distorted and I heard her say that they would be in town week after next to see me. Then the phone cut off. Houdini crossed his legs in the back and his black eyes were in my rearview mirror.

"Here. I hate that song." I pushed the radio dial to the next station. I looked back. He shook his head. Then I pushed it to the next. This Houdini was tricky. The song came in. "Galileo" by the Indigo Girls.

"How long before a soul gets it right?" I asked Houdini.

Natalie turned to me but she looked different, too. "What do you mean?" Her lips changed and began to shimmer.

Scared. "Get the fuck out of my backseat!"

"What are you talking about Piper?"

"Nothing. Do you know how to kick box, Natalie?"

"Where did that come from?"

"Nowhere." Then I mumbled, "That's the spirit."

I pulled the car over to the next exit—Mineral, Virginia. A small town in between somewhere and nowhere. Natalie complained that it would take us till tomorrow to get to Richmond. But, I needed another message. Mineral. Maybe I'd run into an alchemist and get another message. This school-basketball thing was trifling and nebulous compared to what it was I was supposed to do. Fuck school. Fuck basketball. Fuck Mandy Weaver.

Walking into the truck stop diner, I noticed the top ten list on the wall of favorite foods and attitudes. Good message. Then David Letterman was behind the cash register ringing up the line of people buying Snowballs, Tootsie Rolls, cans of Coke and twelve-packs of beer. Number one on the top ten list was to sing your order if you wanted ten percent off. Sing your order?

Three men in wheelchairs rolled by me and swung into a table near the window. I watched as the waitress came up and each one started howling off-key about cheeseburgers and french fries and s-w-e-e-e-t t-e-e-a-a.

Just outside the diner, I saw a police car and two officers hand-cuffing a dark-haired man. Houdini. I caught his eye and he winked at me. The three men in wheelchairs stopped their ordering and all at the same time stared at me. The diner was silent. All at once, their eyes turned to crosses. When I turned to see what David Letterman was doing, I saw him slowly remove his glasses and then the same happened to him: crosses.

Religion. Exorcism. 666. Prophets. Apostles. My brain became electric as the messages began to pour in. I didn't even have to look for them. They were all there, coming faster than my brain could conjugate them.

"What took you so long?" Natalie asked as I got back in the truck. I had a twelve-pack of beer, a Seventies disco CD, a stolen menu and David Letterman's glasses.

"There was a long line and some guys in wheelchairs asked me a bunch of questions. Here, I bought this CD for you."

"Thanks. They asked you a bunch of questions?" Natalie opened the CD. "Like what?"

"Like how long do you think it will take to spring Harry?"

"Harry?"

"Houdini."

"I thought Houdini was dead."

I stopped the truck. "Natalie, Houdini is dead. But sometimes people can reinvent themselves even long after they've given up on this life. You know, it's never too late in life or death to revise."

"Piper. Is your grandfather going to be as weird as you?"

"My grandfather is going to give me the fucking key."

"To what?"

"To life."

"Your grandfather has the key to life? How's that, Piper?"

"Because when you take away life by fault, you find the key by default."

"Okay, whatever that means? You want to hear this CD? It looks cool."

"That's the spirit, Natalie! Pop it in."

The first song had a message. It was Elton John's "Daniel." *Traveling tonight on a plane.* Look out for red tail lights. Okay. Got it.

In the sun with your dress undone came the message from "Thunder Island." Dresses? I hated dresses. Making love out on Thunder Island. Where was Thunder Island?

"Wow, these are some old songs." Natalie rolled her window down. "Looks like we might get some rain." She pointed to the clouds ahead. Her white-blond hair wafted in the wind. Her long V-neck black shirt annealed tightly to her small breasts and her jeans rode low on her waist.

"Do you mind if we go somewhere before we go to Shockoe Sallie's?" I asked. I checked my rearview mirror. Then the angels came back in my head and the clanging reverberated.

"Like where?" she asked.

"The intersection where my family died." I looked her way.

"Sure, whatever you need. I know it must be hard—"

I checked the rearview mirror and got a wink. This time it was a pretty blond lady who looked tired and sullen. I did not recognize who she was. Then her eyes made crosses and when I glanced away and then back again she was gone.

"So, do you think we'll do okay in next week's classic tournament?"

"What tournament?" I asked.

"The classic tournament, silly. Don't you remember? Aren't your folks coming in for it?"

"Yes." I thought, *Hmmm.* The tournament. Magnanimous. Good sign, Natalie. "You think I'll get any playing time?"

"You've got a great shot and you're fast. I think Saneha is going to start. You may fill in when Coach P. pulls her out. Especially if she gets an attitude. You know how Saneha is."

"Yeah. She's got an attitude. I like her, though. She's pretty funny off court. Especially when she mocks Coach Potter and how she talks with her hands and arms like she's flailing around like a chicken. Or a banshee, or a dervish." I checked my rearview mirror again. Coast clear.

"That is funny. Potter's a funny bird. You know she's so far in the closet that it's become a running joke to bet on when she will come out. Everyone knew last year that she was seeing Mandy, except for her and Mandy. You could tell. Plus Nikki and Theonia and Jessie and I staked-out Coach P.'s place one night. Early on Sunday, guess who walked out the back door and lip-locked onto Coach Potter— no resuscitation involved. I'd be careful with Mandy, Piper. She was really hurt at the end of last season and everyone knew why. Coach Potter can be mean. Like when she made Saneha clean her locker out like she had kicked her off the team. Mean. She's tricky."

"I have to pee," I stated.

"Again? How much further?"

"Twenty minutes?"

"You can't wait twenty minutes?"

"Well. Maybe."

So, we rolled along.

When we got to Richmond, it didn't take long to get to the intersection near Carver Middle School on Otterdale Road where my parents and brother died. Beyond the flashing lights and then the stoplight was Lucky's convenience store where my dad and grandfather had bought beer and cigarettes and milk on occasion. There was a sharp slope as the crossroad neared and I pulled over to the edge of the road just across the end of Scout's bridge near a sparse line of pine trees. Natalie opened her car door and put her sunglasses on.

Staring at the tarred, concrete intersection, I mustered the courage to get out and inspect it. I brought along one of my spiral notebooks and a blue ink pen and leaned against my truck. Careful not to miss a point, I sketched the entire intersection. The hilly roadside with sparse patches of tired grass gave way to the concrete sidewalk. I was pretty sure they were driving north on Otterdale Road as it intersected with Gaskins Road. How many times had I played the inconceivable scene in my head? More now as I got older so I could maintain the fathomability of it. Not one. Not two. But all three. Dead. Dead. Dead.

Like a gun it went off in my head. Head. Head. Head.

My brain was on fire. I held it.

The fire raced in my brain traveling like red ants marching to war.

I spat on the ground near the curved edge of the intersection where I was sure the truck had landed gnarled and smashed like an accordion. People drove by the intersection and slowed to see who I was and what I was doing. I drew. I drew it out like I thought it should be. But how could you draw the fear. How do you draw fear?

"You okay?" Natalie asked as she came up from behind me.

I turned around. "Yeah. Can you pick up some sticks for me?"

"What?"

"Sticks. I need six sticks. Can you find them about this long?" I gave an imaginary eight-inch measurement by separating my index fingers.

"Sure. Be right back."

There wasn't any twine in the truck, but I had some athletic tape I used for my ankles. Natalie sat down next to me and helped me make three crosses with ankle tape to bind them together. It was all I had. As we bound them, a man and a woman came along the sidewalk. He was in a wheelchair and had sunglasses on. His hair was dark and cut neatly. The woman was tall with mousy brown hair and impish looking. She had on aviator glasses. Both were wearing almost matching outfits: khaki pants and white button-down shirts. She had a sweater tied around her neck.

Instinctively, I waved at them and smiled. "How are you?"

"Fine, thanks. How are you?" They both said it simultaneously.
"Good. Nice day."

"You need some help with that?" the man asked and pointed to my sloppy attempt at trying to make a cross for my brother.

"I think I got it. But thanks anyway," I said.

Natalie blurted out. "You have a knife? It would help if we had a knife."

The man in the chair rolled to the edge of the grass and then reached around to the pouch clipped to the side and pulled out an army knife. "This ought to do the trick. Here, hand me the one you're working on."

I handed Jack's cross to the man. He cut the white tape on the inside corners to even it out, then cut the edges of the cross on each end piece to even it up.

"Will you do my dad's?" I asked handing him the next one.

"Sure thing."

For the next twenty minutes he and his wife helped even out the tape and smooth out the edges. He had a spoon on the end of the knife, so Natalie helped me dig three holes in the ground.

"How did you get in the chair?" I asked finally.

"Bad fall on a horse," he said. "Nearly killed me but I'm not complaining. I've got the best woman alive to support me." He held his hand out to his wife's and she grasped it.

She looked at me. "Who were these people to you, honey?"

"My whole family—my mother, father and brother," I said. When I looked at her, she had taken her glasses off and her eyes turned to crosses. I looked away because it scared me.

"It's okay, honey," she said while cupping her hand on my shoulder.

Natalie finished the last hole and everyone helped me put the crosses in the ground.

"Everywhere I drive," I said finally. "Everywhere I drive, I see markers of where people have died and flowers and names engraved. All I have is tape and sticks. It isn't special. Special . . ." I held my mouth.

"The feeling is special," the blond lady said, putting her hand on my shoulder. "It's the feeling, honey. That's all. Plus you came here. How long has it been since they passed?"

I looked away from her and at the man in the wheelchair. "How long has it been since you passed?"

They were silent.

They put their sunglasses back on and rolled down the small ridge to the walkway. Moving slowly toward Scout's bridge, the man put his thumb up in the air for me to see.

I spat on the ground to purify it. Then dropped my pants and peed on the ground.

"Jesus Christ, Piper, get your ass up! What in the hell are you doing? For Christ's sake, you are going to get us arrested. Pull your pants up. Pull your pants up. What's wrong with you?"

"I'm scared, Natalie. I'm scared. I'm so fucking scared." I burst into tears and lay down on the grass next to the three markers. "I've never been so scared in my whole life."

Natalie was shaking and she put her hands down on me. "What are you scared of? What is it that has you acting weird and scared? You're beginning to scare me. All I wanted to do was come to Richmond and go to a gay bar and dance and now you're peeing on the ground and acting goofy. Do you want me to call Mandy? Would it help if Mandy was here?"

"Yes. Call Mandy. I need her. Tell her I need her." I put my head back on the ground. Natalie grabbed her cell phone from the car and called her.

"Tell her I can't do it without her. I need her with me."

"Do what without her?"

"Change the world."

"Oh shit. Now I'm really scared. How the hell are you going to change the world, Piper?"

"One notebook at a time. I have a lot of figuring to do." I spat on the ground and then looked to the pine trees on the edge of the road. The needles shook in the wind. Exactly, I thought.

"She's not answering. I'm going to leave her a message and then I think you and me need to get a drink."

"I need to see Victor," I replied. "There's beer in my backpack."

"You are wearing me out. Okay. But we aren't staying long. Where's your cell phone?"

"In my backpack with the beer."

Natalie unzipped my pack. "Holy cow! How many notebooks do you have in here? This backpack weighs a ton." Natalie took out my phone and punched Teeter's number. "Teeter, call me when you get a chance. Piper wants to change the world and all I want is a cold drink." She rolled her eyes at me. "This is my nine-one-one call to you. Help! Call back!" She flipped it shut and exhaled strongly.

"Someday was in my dreams last night, you know," I said.

Natalie sat down beside me and opened me a warm beer.

Swallowing hard, I continued, "She was in my truck and I couldn't get her out. I had to write this guy a check to get her out and every time I went to write the numbers, they came out all screwed up. My name looked different on all the checks. I put a smiley face on one. Then after about twenty checks, I found myself in my old apartment calling my mother and asking her to help me get Someday out of the truck."

"What happened?" Natalie cracked open another beer. I was surprised the police hadn't arrived yet.

"I looked out the bay window of the apartment where I used to live and Someday was running around the cul-de-sac chasing a rabbit."

"Your mom got her out of the truck?"

"I don't know. But she was free."

"That's a good thing. I know you miss them. Everyone on the team knows you miss your dog. We thought it was funny that you wouldn't come down here unless they let your dog come. Then once we saw you two together, we understood. Have you thought about getting a puppy?"

"No. I don't think I'll be able to do that till forever is over. It'll be too hard."

"Forever is a long time."

"There is not time in forever. That's the point."

"Oh, I never thought of it that way." She chugged her beer. "Come on, let's get out of this place before we get into trouble and have to run four gazillion suicides in reverse on Monday."

"Okay. Can we just stop by the VA for a few minutes to see Victor?"

"You're buying all the beer at Shockoe Sally's then." Natalie trotted ahead of me to the truck.

"You got it!"

The wooden crosses in the ground were a tad askance, so I straightened them up. Three crosses at the intersection near Scout Bridge—another sign. The difference here was that I made these signs—all three of them.

My spirit felt broken.

A train passed in the distance.

Where was everyone hiding?

Where was my bridge to cross?

Natalie drove to the VA hospital and talked about basketball the entire way. I focused on some of her words but the air was sticky with white fog that closed in on my line of peripheral vision. Words floated against the dashboard and the songs on the radio gave me more messages than I could hold in. At one point, Natalie's cell rang and I heard Mandy's voice on the receiver saying she couldn't come and that she didn't want to talk to me. My palms got sweaty and I wiped them fervently on my jeans. Natalie stopped at Lucky's convenience store and purchased a carton of cigarettes and a case of beer.

Before getting to the VA, I smoked four cigarettes and gurgled down three beers. Something had to get this nonsense out of me. There was no conjugating any of it anymore. Time to get drunk. Getting drunk always helped.

When we arrived, I spotted Harry Williams in the hallway resting in his wheelchair with his head on his hand. Feeling buzzy, I decided to cut right to the chase when I approached him. Placing the baseball cap on my head, I annealed the Velcro just so and pulled my hair through the adjustor band hole. The brim was tight and low on my forehead.

"How was the meeting with Bobby Kennedy?" I asked him. It had been nearly two months since my last visit.

"I didn't go."

"Why?"

"I'm going to the bathroom," Natalie said, then scurried down the hall.

"I don't know." Harry Williams looked at me. "Have we met?"

"I think we can get your brother soon. I'll try and reach him."

"How are you going to do that?"

"Same way you reach who you want to reach."

"Oh, I see!" He tapped his head and smiled. "Soon very soon. We need to get his friend Chris here, too."

"Who's Chris?"

"You know." I tapped my head.

"Oh, okay." And he tapped his back. "They've paid for our passages, you know."

"What?"

"The Kennedys have paid for our passage . . . today. Here. Now."

The clock read twenty-two past the hour. "Yes, I believe they have, too."

Meandering down the hall I became nervous and confused. People's eyes were on me and I felt naked, like they were seeing through me. Fuck. I started my internal cacophony of feeling. Numb. Scintillating. Galvanizing. Then, of course, fuck again.

The same nurse from the last visit noticed me and started my way from around the nurses' station.

"Are you here to see Victor Cliff?" she asked and then looked me up and down. "You okay?"

"Yes, I am." Perhaps I was visibly shaking. I was scared talking to her and then her lips turned slick and slippery. Fuck again.

"Well, he's very tired and I think you agitated him the last time . . ."

"No. I think I agitated you," I said.

"He's doped up a bit—"

"Who isn't dopey in this place?"

"I don't have to let you in, you know," she said and began to walk away.

Ignoring her, I walked into Victor's room. Lying under the sheets, he had a book on his chest. I couldn't make out what it was, so I stepped closer. It was *The Awakening* by Kate Chopin. It was the biggest sign of the day.

Victor's face was more drawn and pinched than the last time— frailer, too. Although I felt squeamish sitting, I did so anyway. The movement of the chair stirred him and he turned his head from the window and regarded me.

"How's the book," I said finally.

"Oh, this. Pretty good. Your friend Vera sent it to me when I asked her what you were studying in school. She's a smartie, that woman."

"Yeah. Being an ex-librarian and all helps, I think."

"You okay? You look tired."

"Yeah."

"How's basketball? You knocking 'em through the hoop?"

"A bit. We've had a couple of games to start the season. We have our big classic tournament coming up after fall exams. Fall exams. Fall exams. We play UVA, VCU and ODU." I put my hand over my mouth.

"How do the Cavaliers look?"

"They're always good. Debbie Ryan has a decent program. We're playing in the new John Paul Jones Arena. Should be a good crowd right before the holidays."

"You playing?"

"No, not much. Saneha Tomlinson is the number one girl in my position. She plays pretty much the whole game. I'll be lucky if I get a few minutes here and there."

"Well, that's all right. You read this book?"

"Not yet."

"It's pretty good. Has a lot of French names in it that I can't pronounce so I just skip over them." He picked the book up off his chest and pulled his reading glasses from off his chest. "Well, let me see here. I just read something a little while ago that I thought you might like . . ."

While he fumbled, I looked out the window then slicked my hair back with the palms of my hands and recapped myself. Someday came to me in my mind. I saw her standing near my father in the woods near the pier. Now, I was eyeing the man who'd fathered my father. Who was paying for whose passage? I could hear Someday whine. And then, boom, the clanging noise started from right outside Victor's door.

"Jesus! Where did that come from?" I asked looking right at Victor.

"It's here on page one hundred and four. Listen. Let me read it to you. 'The artist must possess the courageous soul that dares and defies.' Isn't that a good line? 'Dares and defies.' I like that. Do you?"

"Say it again. Did you hear that noise?" I gazed for a moment through the window. The oily, furry smell of my dog was on my hands. I slicked back my hair and stared at my grandfather and tried to concentrate.

Natalie walked by and waved. She had on her sunglasses.

Bang. The clanging came again.

"'The artist must possess the courageous soul that dares and defies.'"

"That's a good line. I like it."

"I'm not sure what the rest of the book is trying to say but that's the prettiest line I've read so far. Vera told me not long ago that you like to read—"

"Yes. I write some, too."

"Oh, a writer, are we? What do you write?"

"Nothing. I just write nothing."

"Oh, now, don't say that. A smart girl like you. Well, I bet you write some good lines just like this Chopin woman does."

I adjusted myself in my seat and then fidgeted for a moment. I slicked my hair back again then got up and walked to the window. "I went to the intersection today, Victor. I made wooden crosses. Did you send that man there?"

"What man?"

"The man in the wheelchair. Did you send him?"

"No, honey. I didn't send anyone there. I didn't even know you were going. You all right? You look tired and extra skinny."

There was a long silence and then Victor cleared his throat like he was preparing a speech.

"I know you know what happened that night, Piper. You figured that one out long ago."

"Victor—" The clanging sounded again. "We don't need to talk about it—"

"Now hold on. We do. It's high time and I'm not going to be around much longer to tell you some of these things. So, you just have to let me. Let me tell my war and perhaps a little of my peace. Okay?"

"Go ahead." I stared through the window, then my eyes began to burn. Across the road to the VA hospital stood a man, a woman, a boy and a dog.

Victor placed the book on his bed stand and tried to sit up. Smoothing the sheets out, he cleared his smoky throat. "I know you know what happened to your mother, my son and my grandson. Even now—" He hesitated. "Even now, I feel so guilty, I can barely speak of it. I did the worst thing imaginable. I took life. Not one. Not two. But three." He swallowed down his pain.

"I know," I said. "You never even went to jail."

"My jail has been different. I haven't been behind bars or served time for what I did. But, I tell ya, my mental anguish has been so hot. So hot that sometimes I had to hold my head for minutes, sometimes longer just to find relief. I know this might not make you feel any better. I sat at my kitchen table for years with my head on it. Just sat like that staring out the kitchen window waiting to die. I let you go because I thought if I wiped all of you out of my head then it would empty itself and I would somehow feel better. I'm sorry, little girl. I'm sorry I gave you up. I'm sorry for what I did. I can't change what happened, you know. I've been suffering over it my whole life. I quit drinking when this lady came to the house one day selling religion."

"Did you buy it?"

"What?"

"The religion. Did you buy it?" I looked at him.

"No. I've never been much on it. But she sat down at the table with me for a while. She washed my dishes, gave me her business card and then left."

"She washed your dishes? This made you stop drinking?" I was confused.

He looked away for a moment, then looked back. "She just helped me a little. That was it. She just helped me a little. That was it. A week later, I was in the same position and I just started staring at her card then I called her."

"Did she remember you?"

"Yes. I asked her if she could drive me to a doctor. She did. She came and got me and drove me to a clinic. That was that."

"That was how you stopped drinking."

"Yep."

"So, it didn't take fucking everything else up. Just some washed dishes and a card from a Jehovah's Witness?"

He shifted again. "Well, little girl, I guess that's the most of it. She was just the little I needed."

"I remember washing your dishes. You and your friend, Clover, would eat and drink and I would wash dishes every morning while you all were passed out in front of the TV."

"Clover's dead, you know. Drowned in the James River last year near the pier where we all used to fish. I think he fell off the bridge trying to unhook a fish and was too drunk to make it out. Only five feet of water and he drowned."

I soaked this one in for a moment. "So, you've been talking to Vera?" I had been wondering.

"Yes, I've called to speak with your foster parents and she's usually the one who answers the phone."

"She's pretty cool. She's gay, you know." I kept staring at the people across the road. I thought of the paratrooper and his cat Leon and wondered how her little paw was doing.

"That's all right. Gay people are all right," he said and pulled the covers up around his chest.

"You didn't used to think so."

"Well, in life sometimes you have to go through some shit to understand some shit. Know what I mean?"

He laughed and I laughed too—actually, a true guffaw. It was the first time at all that I could remember doing anything pleasing together. Laughing with my grandfather for a minute. His eyes got brighter and I realized suddenly and without hesitation that his journey was my journey—that both our spirits had nearly been broken by the weight of it all. I was me because of what he went through. The hardness, the longing, the fucked up feelings . . . all of it was as in me as it was in him. The epiphany resounded in my broken heart.

At this point, I wasn't sure if I should hug him or just pat him on the leg or something. As I walked to the edge of the bed, his laughter subsided and his eyes were burning a bit like mine had been staring out the window looking at the family across the road.

"Someday died, you know," I said moving closer. "She was such a good girl."

"Sit down here," he said patting the bed. "You and that damn dog were inseparable. I remember. I know you loved her, honey."

He put his hand on my forearm and I let it rest there. We did not speak for a while. Then we slid our hands down to meet and we held each other's palms. Holy palms.

Eventually, Natalie appeared in the doorway and I could tell she was fed up with my ritualistic behavior. She leaned against the doorframe and crossed her arms. The signal, evidently that it was time to go.

As I squeezed my grandfather's palms, his eyes turned to crosses, but it did not scare me so much this time. "The artist must possess what? What did the author say?"

He smiled. "The courageous soul that dares and defies."

It was his message. I got it loud and clear.

Chapter 11

At Blue Ridge Medical Center, the time changed in the world as six billion darkly cloaked people, like small falling dominoes, all laid their heads down to sleep. Every minute of the day millions of people lying down to sleep. No wonder the earth turned on its axis. All that lying down caused the world to spin around and around—little bubbles of air seeping out from under the arch of the neck to spark a wind that would catch onto the next and then the next. Time was touchable in the surreal night of nights, in the day of days. How the world changed every day!

I was ready to conjugate the fear now, expunge the anxiety. It was time. The snake was near and my womanifesto was out, out, out and into the world! John Paul Jones Arena had seen this artist courageous and daring. The great John Paul Jones Arena! The Tell-Tale brain had spun itself right into the crowd! What a sight it had been! A great awakening! The dreams were beginning. Through it all, I would make my parents proud—they would catch it in the spirited, breathy air. I knew it. It was as deep as the red in the stained glass in a church on every Sunday. Not just last Sunday—but for all of the Sundays. I would make my parents and my brother see through the gossamer air. We would touch through the air! We would touch once more!

Out in the foyer of the ward in the lounge area, Jenny and Vera and Andrea had called but I could not remember what they said. Their words sounded like gouflexed-shroida, garbled and gnarled.

Rose came out of our room. She held a glass case where the snake was lying in wait to bite me to create the next step in this world-changing event. It didn't know that I was going to bite it first then eat the son of a bitch.

Lynn asked if I wanted to smoke because everyone was going in. I told her I would be there in a minute. I was too busy eyeing Rose as she walked down the corridor and out of sight. Where was she going?

Dickey Dred sat down next to me and I told him to move. Fuck off he said but I didn't listen.

John Kennedy rolled his wheelchair next to the chair where I was sitting.

"It won't be long," I said.

"Long for what?"

"We're going to get a cure for what you've got."

"What? Being in this chair?"

"Yes. It won't be long."

"Good. I'm sick of being in this position."

"I kept looking for the holy palms, you know. The ones that Christopher Reeve told Robin to tell me to look for. He said they would be by my bed. And they were. My grandfather showed me the holy palms."

"Okay." He wheeled closer. "Can I help you with anything? I keep seeing this little guy, Jack. I think his name is Jack. He keeps telling me to hold onto my head. I'm not sure what that means."

"Me neither. But it's good information." Then I leaned my head on the side of the chair to wait for the clanging to come. Buster crinkled up his newspaper in the corner of the room and people of all ages began to come through the doors. They were here to see the conjugation, I guess. They were here to witness the venom that would cure the ailments that ailed them. Today we were getting a throat-hold on the killers of the two girls from Spotwood County and the cure for paralysis. Two birds with one stone. Two birds with one snake.

Vera sat down next to me and gave me some chewing gum. "Here, you want some?"

"Yes." I pulled a piece from the wrapper and crammed it into my mouth. Peppermint.

When I looked at her and smiled, her face turned ghostly white and small angels hovered near the portal to her ears. "Joan? Joan of Arc?"

"Do you see Joan of Arc? Do you think I'm J of A?" She laughed.

Her words swirled like gold dust around the J and the A. Her voice deepened . . . I looked up and saw that the gauntlet had arrived. Harry Houdini melded nicely into Robin Williams like they were Siamese twins. Then Bobby Kennedy held onto Hilary Swank. On the carpet, the foursome formed a kind of arch, then they put their feet together, toe to toe facing one another. Then the portal to heaven opened beneath the fire red Exit sign: ROSE. Rose came in with the glass case. Her arms were wrapped around it so that I could not see the snake in it. I gripped Joan of Arc . . . her muscles were strong and vibrant. Andrea and Jenny held hands to the left side of the gauntlet and their eyes were on me. They knew of the womanifesto and its power. I was scared. Scared. Scared. I held my urine. I held it. I held it. I held. Hold. Hold. Hold. Hold . . .

Then the bridge formed and the train raced across and sounded its clanging horn. From miles away, I could hear the chug-a-chug . . . and the clanging of the church bell that tolled six miles from that. Then the arch of the bridge cracked open and the spirits of my family broke through. The spirits of my family broke through. The spirits of my family broke through. They did not break down. They broke up. Free and away. Across the bridge from my childhood, across the bridge at the VA hospital, across the bridge of the world. They were breaking through. They were breaking through. Through. Through.

And, then, I was though. Some channel in my brain broke away . . .

The clanging was in my heart. I'd been hearing its quiet crescendo since the day they died. It was in me, not out there.

Rose approached me and sat in the chair across from me. "You okay, Piper?" she asked.

"Yes."

Andrea and Jenny sat down next to J of A. Jenny opened a magazine and Andrea fiddled with her cell phone.

Andrea clipped it to her side and exhaled. "So, daughter, you want to go outside for a little bit? You've got some friends here who want to see you but they aren't allowed up here."

"Rose? Do you want me to take that from you?" I asked.

"What? This box?"

"Yeah, I need to eat the snake." I trembled and J of A squeezed my hand.

Vera put her strong, veiny hands on my face and turned me toward her. She smiled at me. Her eyes danced and her chubby face looked beautiful. "Piper, you don't have to eat the snake, honey. We've read some of your writings in your womanifesto. Andrea and Jenny and me have been reading that great work of yours the last day or two. You have some great ideas, honey. But, eating a snake isn't one of them. You're mixed up and confused and sick. Rightfully so, who wouldn't be a little messed up if you'd lost your whole family and then you leave your home in Canada to come back to Virginia. The scene of the crime, if you will. Mine, too, by the way. And, then, you've lost your dog. She was your link to life. But, I'm telling you as sure as me and Andrea and Jenny are sitting here, so are your mom and dad and Jack and Someday. Let Someday take care of the snakes for you now, Piper. She was always your guardian, you know. Let her stay that way. Okay?"

"Joan?"

"No, I'm not Joan, honey. It's Vera. But Joan and me have a lot in common . . . we both want to fight for what is good and right till the day we die. And, Piper, you are good and right."

Jenny leaned in. "We're going to get you well, Piper. If you need me and Andrea to kick the shit out of some of your demons, then we're here to do so."

"There's a snake in the case Rose is holding. I'm supposed to eat it."

Andrea looked at Rose. "Rose, do you mind if we have a look in your case?"

"No, here." She handed the box to Jenny who was now up and standing next to her.

"If I eat the snake, we will find the cure for paralysis . . . I have to eat it." I was upset and did not know what to do.

Vera held onto my shoulders. "You don't have to find the cure for paralysis, Piper. It's you. You're paralyzed from the trauma in your head. Your head is paralyzed in the tired state of affairs that it is in."

Andrea stood up and reached into the box. She pulled out something long and red. "It's a scarf! See? It's a red scarf." She put it around her neck and modeled it for us. Jenny laughed at her. I laughed at Jenny.

What was the world coming to?

Jenny stopped and then sat down next to me. "We are sad. No, we are very sad that your mind has been playing tricks on you. I know we may not make sense sometimes. But we don't want to lose you. It's worse than death if you lose your mind." Jenny wrapped her arms around me and burst into tears. "It's worse than death, honey. I know . . . I've been there. I saw it happen to my grandmother. They put her away, you know. They put her into one of those places no one ever talks about and nobody ever saw or spoke of her again. I don't want to lose you. I adopted you and you are my very sweet daughter. Nothing is going to hurt you anymore."

Andrea came in from the side. "That's right. Listen to Jenny. I hope you can hear what she's saying, honey. You're going to come out of this, we know. Hang on. Hang on."

This part of the conjugation was screwing me up. I was ready to eat the snake or the scarf or whatever it was. Now, Jenny was talking about her grandmother and Vera was akin to Joan of Arc. Teeter might be able to help these people as they were confusing the hell out of me.

What about changing the world? Had it not happened at the tournament?

Ten thousand people had witnessed my rebirth.

Chapter 12

Just after exams, our team played in the annual classic tournament. It was one of the biggest season predictors of how teams might do in the NCAA tournament if all players stayed healthy and consistent. I had seen minimal playing time against East Tennesse State University and Farleigh Dickinson College. Saneha was playing well and I only went in when she needed to settle down after a long run. I had gotten in long enough to run up and down the court and pass the ball and get into the rhythm of defense, but in both games, a foul was committed in the middle of my moment and that allowed Saneha to get checked right back in.

It was the second Friday in December and we had to ride across town to play the tournament on UVA's playing court: John Paul Jones Arena. It was BRU's first time playing in an arena that size. When UVA played our intercity rivalry at our venue, it was the same old field house that sat only about two thousand people. John Paul

Jones was huge, with seating of at least ten thousand. The tournament was a big crowd draw because UVA, ODU and VCU were big Division I schools.

Teeter was seeing more playing time this season, and the crowd loved her when she did her "Teetery" hands in the air after she made each shot. So much so, that the cheerleaders began to imitate it and the crowd was beginning to catch on.

Coach Potter saw some amusement in it, too. She wasn't seeing any amusement in me, however, since I was doing poorly in school and had missed two practices because of going to Richmond to see Victor. Coach DuPont took up for me, though, and said they were cutting me some slack on account of my dog dying and that once we got back from winter break then things should be back on track. After that—no slack cut.

When we arrived in the arena off the shuttle bus, I made sure I had all of my stuff in my bag that I needed in case I got the high sign. Looking for the right sign had been what I was waiting for before I could really let the world know about my womanifesto. I knew it was coming. It was coming sooner than I thought. And, when I got the sign, I would release the womanifesto for the world to see. The calculations, the geography, the poetry, the links to the earth and sun, the celebrities apparently involved in the cause to cure paralysis—it was all in the spiral notebooks. The tarot cards I was beginning to learn were in there, too. My studies on them had included three trips to a psychic and three trips back to where Mandy and I first kissed up on Route 20.

"Piper, come on." Mandy looked at me. "You okay?"

We were unloading and I was behind the bus looking at a billboard that said something about a new wireless plan. As I was scribbling the note in my newest notebook, Mandy had quietly come up from behind me.

"Fine. And you? How's Coach Potter treating you? Has she made any chest passes at you lately or does she just dribble?"

"You're getting loud." Mandy put her bag on the ground and zipped up her jacket. Putting her hands in her pocket she stepped closer to me. "I want to see you again. I miss you."

"You see me at practice every day." I folded my notebook and put it in my backpack. The Bible and my tarot cards were at the surface.

"Are you doing tarot cards now?" she asked as she peeked in my bag.

"Yes, I am."

Jessie Holmstead came around the back of the bus. "You two better hurry. We're going in."

"We'll be right there," Mandy said. "I know I see you at practice, but I want to see you more."

"You said you needed time away, right?" I stepped off the curb and zipped up my backpack. "This feels like some weird scene out of *The Great Gatsby*. You're coming back after what seems like ten years."

"Piper, quit exaggerating. It's been two, maybe three weeks. You just started acting so weird."

I zipped my jacket up and put my sunglasses on. "You want me to read your tarot cards after the game? I flipped Teeter and Kara and Theonia out last night after we played ping. Theonia got this sword card with all the swords stuck in this man's back and neck and she thought that I doing some kind of voodoo on her. She had to run and call her mom to make sure she was okay. It was hysterical."

"I don't think that's funny."

"Teeter called her folks too. But she got good cards."

"Teeter called her folks?"

"Yeah. They live in Earlysville, I think."

"Piper. Teeter's folks are dead. She didn't tell you?"

"No shit." This was clearly ominous. I pushed my sunglasses up. "I think this must be it."

"What?"

"Never mind. We need to get inside, I guess."

"Will you read my cards after the game? I think it would be cool. Maybe you could drive me up one of the roads you like so much and we could drink a beer. What do you think?"

"I think you two need to get your butts inside." It was Coach Potter standing with arms akimbo around the front side of the bus. "Mandy, can I talk to you?"

We both picked up our respective bags and walked toward Coach Potter. Looking beyond her and out and into the street, I saw a girl in jeans and a sweater looking my way. She had dark hair and her dog had a bandage around his back leg. Suddenly, and without any thought, I dropped my bag and ran across the street toward them.

"Hey," I said as I approached. She was stopped on the corner. Her dog sat down.

"How did your dog get hurt?" I glanced down the street and saw a tall black man with salt-and-pepper hair approaching. He had on aviator glasses and walked briskly.

The girl smiled. "Oh, she was this way when I got her. I just rescued her last week from the SPCA. I am giving her to my brother for Christmas." She leaned down and patted the golden Lab mix on the head.

"What's her name? Have you named her?"

Coach Potter yelled from across the street. "You better get your butt back over here. I need to talk to you, Piper."

"For now, I'm calling her Goldie. She's a golden girl. You have a dog?"

"Yeah. Her name is Someday. She's in heaven."

"Oh, I'm sorry to hear that."

Coach Potter yelled for me again.

"That's okay. Heaven's only about twenty-six miles away from here."

The girl laughed. I saluted Nelson Mandela who came upon us and then bells tolled from the church behind us.

"It's time!" I yelled and skipped back across the street to where Coach Potter and Mandy were standing. Running past them, I yelled, "It's time!"

Racing into the locker room, I quickly whispered into Teeter's ear that it was time. She told me to shut up and get dressed. Shifting my notebooks around, I made a few more scribblings in one and then closed it up. I put on my uniform and my warm-up suit and buttoned the shirt up the wrong way. Then I put on my sunglasses.

Kara looked at me. "Take those things off. What do you think this is, a rock concert or something?"

I smiled at her. "Bright lights." Her eyes turned to crosses. It was then that I felt a little scared as to what I was about to do. But, I'd seen all of them. Heard all of them.

After warm-ups, we sat down on the bench. VCU was going to be a difficult opponent for us since they were twice as big and had two all-Americans leading the starting five. Coach Potter gave us the typical coaching speech about how we had to move our feet, look for one another and play loose. Find your man and stay with them, she said like, four times, looking for her next point to make. The veins in her head and neck stuck out and I caught her looking at Mandy and Mandy looking at her. My stomach dropped an abysmal million miles. I thought that that goofy feeling was over.

We high-fived in the middle of the group and then after the announcements, the game got underway. Coach DuPont scanned the crowd and said there was a good turnout. I speculated the same and then saw the wheelchair section. I could not take my eyes off the people sitting there and then I saw one with a service dog on the corner aisle across the arena. I tried to pay attention to the game, but couldn't help but just look over at them every chance I got.

Teeter made a shot and then did her Teeter hand dance and the crowd from BRU roared. Coach Potter mimicked her and everyone loved that, too. At 12:22 left on the clock in the first half, Saneha made two impeccable steals for down-the-court layups and was losing her wind. Potter called me to come down to her end. Kara grabbed my sunglasses and told me to pay attention.

Potter grabbed my shorts. "Okay, Piper, I need you to go in for Saneha and keep the offense going for a few minutes. Make sure you ask Saneha who her man is when you check in. Make a difference out there. Got it?"

"Like I've never had it before!" I yelled.

"Good. Now go in and keep the rhythm going. I'm watching

you. This is your chance to shine! Don't mess it up."

My chance to shine. Good words. And, of course I did.

When I checked into the game, everything looked blue and black and everyone's hair seemed to stand on end. It was funny. We were taking the ball inbounds on the sideline closest to the people in the wheelchairs. I stepped outside of the mid-court line to receive the ball from the ref and everything went into slow motion. The clanging started in the rear and I turned my head to look for the source. I saw a man drinking from his cup and when he looked at me, his lips turned to snakes. Fuck.

I'd better hurry, I thought.

"Teeter! Teeter!" I yelled before the ref handed me the ball.

She was pinned up against a girl with her arm outstretched waiting for a potential pass. The ref handed me the ball and started to count with his arm. One. Two. I held the ball at my side.

"Teeter!" I yelled again. She looked at me and for some reason knew something was wrong. Three. I had two seconds. I had two seconds to change the whole fucking world.

"I thought your parents were alive!" I yelled. Four.

On five, instead of throwing the ball inbounds, I threw it to the little girl I had noticed sitting in her wheelchair. To her dismay and mine, she caught it.

"It's HERE! It's here. It's here," I yelled across the arena and ran with my arms in the air all the way to the bench.

Everyone stopped. I had everyone's full attention. Taking my notebooks from my backpack, I ran from corner to corner of the basketball floor and tossed my notebooks into the crowd, all the while yelling, "The cure for paralysis lies in the snake in Brazil! Somebody needs to call Christopher Reeve and tell him."

Teeter was running after me and yelling something but I was too fast for her. I stopped in the middle of the floor and tore the shirt off my body. "Can you hear me, you clanging bells? Because I hear you! It's here. You know it. I know it. It's here. The birds know it. The trees know it. All the signs to help these people are here. You all just need to connect the messages and then the suffering will end.

It's here. It's here."

Coach Potter was yelling. My whole team was standing on the sideline.

"Technical foul. Technical foul." One of the referees was flittering around me using the hand signal for a technical foul. It seemed as if the whole crowd was hanging on my every word. Then I pulled my pants down and began to pee on center court. Teeter grabbed me.

"Piper!" She held me in a bear hug. "What's going on girl? You just lost your shit in front of a lot of people." Two men in security uniforms grabbed my arms.

"You need to read the notebooks Teeter. Someday. Where is she? She's supposed to appear on the sideline in her mascot uniform. Where is she? Where is my little girl, Teeter. She's all I had. I couldn't save her. I couldn't save her. I couldn't save her. Will you read it?" I burbled with tears.

"We need to get you some help, girl." It was all she said.

The men were asking a bunch of questions I did not understand. I was suddenly isolated and everyone was staring at me.

"Teeter. You have to be with me on this . . ." I spat on the floor.

"Piper, you're in serious need of some help. And keep your bodily fluids inside. Damn."

Coach Potter came up with Coach Dupont and they circled me and Teeter. Natalie Wingfield came up from the left side and then Kissie came up from the right.

"Fuck all of you! Let me go. Let me go." I struggled against Teeter.

Coach Potter grabbed me by the shoulder sleeve. "This is it Piper. Get off the floor. Let's go to the locker room with Kissie and get some air. We're done."

"Fuck you! Quit fucking my girlfriend!"

Teeter said, "Uh, oh. Watch your mouth!"

Then I looked to see Mandy standing on the sideline. Her hair stood on end and her hands were on her hips. She didn't look my way.

"Quit fucking her!" I looked at Mandy and everyone turned to look at her.

It took them close to ten minutes to get me off the court and into an ambulance to escort me to Blue Ridge Medical Center.

Chapter 13

Victor died on the Tuesday after I was admitted to the psychiatric ward of Blue Ridge Medical Center. Vera and Jenny and Andrea were there to tell me the news. There were some items he left to me including a mosaic inlaid glass box that contained the wedding bands of both my mother and father and the St. Christopher medal my brother Jack wore before he died. Why they weren't buried with them I don't know. Someday's puppy collar with her first tag that had our home address and phone number on it. There were a few letters and a small savings account with close to fifteen thousand dollars that he left to me for the day I graduated from college or when I got married or had a civil union.

Apparently, my womanifesto made it out to the crowd but Teeter and Kissie and Natalie were able to get most of it back during the few minutes of bedlam at the John Paul Jones Arena.

I never had to conjugate the snake or the scarf it really was. By the

time all the right celebrities were in place for me to eat the snake that
Rose carried in her glass box, the Lithium and Depakote kicked in
and the surreal reality I had been living in began to infuse back into
the reality everyone else was in. I still think that Vera resembles Joan
of Arc but I will not tell her that.

Vera came in with some fruit and we sat in the visiting area for
a while waiting for Jenny and Andrea to come in from Starbucks.
Jenny couldn't live without a large Venti latte ever. It was one of her
bodily fluids, she told me once.

Vera rattled a magazine and put her hand on my leg as we sat. I
looked out the window to the waving trees but did not wave back. I
thought of my drives in the country and landed right in the middle
of kissing Mandy Weaver one hot fall night in the gym.

"Have you talked to Mandy?" I asked.

"No, honey, I haven't." Vera paused and then closed the magazine. "Did you write about her in your womanifesto?"

"Yes."

"Well, then, that's all you need to say, right?"

"I guess."

"You want to look at something I wrote?" she asked, then
smiled.

"Sure. What is it?"

"A poem. It's a poem."

"Read it to me." I curled my legs up and looked at Dickey who
didn't look at all ominous. Uno girl was playing cards and when I
gazed upon her, nothing changed. Not even her eyes.

"You okay?"

"Yeah, why?"

She pulled out an address book in her bag, then a gnarled piece of
paper. "Sometimes when I see you stare, it makes me think you are
seeing things like you did before."

"I'm good. I'm good."

"Okay. Here goes—

'In Canada, there is a pale yellow bird sitting delicate
On the tree branch outside my foggy kitchen window

Flitting its wings back, she regards me like I regard her
Her head softly tilts, my hands stop washing the glass
The quick, quiet bond we make on a Monday morning
Satiates our human nature
I want to stroke her and kiss her but know it is not right
She wants to land on my shoulder and peck at my neck and ears
But feels it is not right
We let each other go into our days
Quick, stop—don't go—I want to say
Stay here with me on my easel of life and I'll fill water for you in this clean
Chalice.'"

I stretched out on the couch and pulled my sweatshirt down and then held onto Vera's hand. "Cool, poem. You're a good writer . . . Vera?" I asked.

"Yes." She folded the poem back and put it into her bag. She pulled her glasses down the bridge of her nose.

"Why am I here?"

"In the hospital?" She looked at me and leaned back.

"No. You know. Why am I here? What am I supposed to do?"

"With what, honey?" She cocked her head to the side.

"Anything?"

"No one knows why we're here. But when it hits you about what you are supposed to do, you'll know," she said, smiling at me.

For a long while, we stayed silent. "I like sparrows, Vera. They're pretty birds," I said.

"I agree. They are pretty."

Paige came into the room and sat down next to me on the couch. Then Dr. Spectrus came out from behind Jackson, the food attendant. Dr. Spectrus said something to Jackson and then Jackson looked at me. He gave a small wave. I waved back.

"Dr. Spectrus has some good news for you, Piper." Paige put her hand on my shoulder. I sat up.

"She's right," Dr. Spectrus said and sat down in a chair next to Vera.

"It looks like we will be stabilizing you here in the next day or so and then you can go home."

Paige squeezed my shoulder. "Isn't that great. You can go home for Christmas!"

"You have had a blending of some psychotic behavior along with a little too much to drink on occasion, eh?" he said, and pushed his Magoo glasses up. "The old term is manic depression; the new one is bipolar. We've discussed this already. Take your medicine. Do not for whatever reason stop your medicine. If you do, you may find yourself wanting to change the world again. And, my lovely patient, that's a lot for one person to do."

Vera looked at me. "Piper, you can change the world if you want to. You might just want to take it down a notch or two."

Everyone laughed but me. Dr. Spectrus scribbled some notes out on a notebook: his manifesto, and then handed it to Vera.

"Can I drive home?" I asked.

"To Banff?" Vera asked.

"Yes. Can I drive home? I know it will take me five days, but I really want to. It's the only thing I want."

"Jesus Christ!" Vera yelled.

Then I laughed.

Chapter 14

On my last day in the hospital, I was still hearing the clanging noises and people's eyes were still messed up. I ran into both Barry and Jerry: aka Bobby and John Kennedy in the smoking room. We smoked three cigarettes in about twenty minutes. Jerry told me that he'd gotten in his wheelchair on a bad diving board accident at the local pool. Barry was a local artist who'd spent his days researching crime scenes for the Fluvanna County police. He said, however, that his job there may be no more since he'd been in the looney bin getting shock therapy treatments. He couldn't keep anything straight in his head. This was a liability on his job. I told him to find the perps or perp who killed those girls in Spotwood County. He said that it was out of his jurisdiction but he would look into it.

Gerald came in looking ghastly as ever and bummed a smoke from me. "You still seeing tricks?" he asked, and exhaled with a fluster and a cold stare into the sterile hospital air.

"You're pretty tricky."

"Just quit calling me Houdini. I already look creepy enough as it is. With that epithet, I'll really scare the staff into one of Stephen King's new horror books."

We all laughed. It was good to laugh.

Then my dumbass roommate walked in.

"Yo, whas up in here?" Teeter walked over and high-fived Barry and Jerry and Robin Wilson who had stumbled in upon the working crime scene in progress.

"Hey, Teeter . . ."

"No, 'hey Teeter, me' . . . I'm here to spring you from this joint. Vera and Andrea and Jenny told me that they were sick of you and told me to come in and launch you right out of here. I hope your medicine is working 'cuz the last time we were in public, I thought I was going to have to knock you out." She balled her fist. "I just fixed my wig . . . so, don't make me run all over the place trying to get your womanifesto out into the public eye. Have you heard of Web sites and Google? These places will help. Okay? Okay."

I said good-bye to all of the celebrities both real and unreal as I left the psychiatric floor. Lynn kissed me on the cheek for good luck and told me that she hoped I'd still find the perps and the cure for paralysis. Dickey Dred told me that sometimes people and things aren't always what they seemed. I told him that he seemed like Nelson Mandela to me. I thought he would kiss me on the lips but he just hugged me instead.

"So, I guess Christopher Reeve and Robin Williams won't show up for the big gig?"

"What big gig?" Teeter asked stopping outside of the front of the hospital. It was cooler outside and I had no jacket.

"Just kidding . . . I still think they're out there with the answers, you know."

Teeter zipped up her jacket. "There are no answers to the questions, Piper. If we knew the answers we wouldn't be trying so hard all the time. You're trying too hard. There's an answer for you."

"You're stupid."

"You're stupider."

From around the corner, the revelation unveiled. Kissie Martin, Kara Featherstone, Natalie Wingfield, Jessie Holmstead, Saneha Jones and Nikki Jackson stood next to my family: Vera Curran, Andrea Black, Jenny Winter. Each one had on a pair of sunglasses. The players were dressed in their BRU blue sport jackets and just to the other side of the bridge was the paratrooper I'd met at the vet when Someday was put down. He was with his family and their dog. Synchronicity? I did not know nor care about either the signs or the meaning.

Breaking Spirit Bridge is the name I would give for the bridges I'd crossed on my travels around Charlottlesville up Route 20 and the drives I'd taken to Richmond to see Victor in the VA hospital. I'd crossed over Jean Noon Bridge, Lee Bridge, Rivanna Bridge, Manchester Bridge, the Freebridge and dozens more. The bridge, to me, that was most important was the one back home in Richmond near my old fort where my young puppy Someday had crossed over years earlier to come and fetch me and my brother to be her guardians . . . she, of course, ours. She seemed to say, hey, come with me. When they all died, including Victor, their spirits had broken through and up and across the bridge of life to death—reborn into a new realm I'd been trying to touch with my heart and my mind for many years. I longed for a glimpse across the bridge to heaven to see them. I longed. I longed. I longed. It was clanging in my soul like the toll of the church bell, the toll of the tires on the road, the toll of the sadness in my own soul. No one should lose life. No one should lose her mind. The fire in my brain was not sending me looking for signs or symbols anymore. I know now that the flesh and bones and river of blood putting my body together are holding onto a spirit much greater than what my small brain can fathom. My spirit had broken through, too.

Now, it was in me. I would spend the rest of my life returning to the place where my family had fished that day and where we had all trudged together as a family across the bridge looking for Someday's beginnings. I now knew that across that bridge near Stoney Creek and the James River was the gateway to heaven on earth. Heaven on earth.

Teeter grabbed my hand. "All these fools want to know if you want to go to the county pound and pick out a puppy."

"Yeah, Piper." Saneha walked up to me. "We think that this team should do everything together. We've decided since your birthday is a few days away that going to the pound to get you a new puppy would be a good thing, eh?" She took her sunglasses off.

Natalie Wingfield sidled up next to me. "As long as you promise to keep your pants up, I'm going, too."

Vera and Jenny and Andrea came close. Vera handed me my backpack. It was lighter.

"We've saved all of your notebooks," Vera said. "I was going to throw them away."

Teeter jumped in. "I wish you would have . . . I had to go and grab them from about a hundred people."

Andrea kissed my forehead. "Piper, keep the notebooks . . . perhaps there is something you can pull together from them that would be helpful for other people who are bipolar."

"It sucks to be bipolar," I said.

"Would you rather be bisexual?" Jessie Holmstead came from around behind me and put her hand on my shoulder.

"Oh, God, not bisexual. Jesus . . . there's a tough one," Jenny argued.

"Bisexual is all right," Teeter said. "I may do that one. Then I'd have the whole phone book to choose from. This wig going to see some action soon."

We laughed.

"What's you all laughing at. Piper, you better get a new notebook. I've got a lot of things I want you to write down for me. It's going to be better than anything you've already conjured up. Guaranteed."

So, we all went to the pound after I said hi to the paratrooper and his wife. They lived nearby and were taking their dog for a walk. No synchronicity. Just happenstance. But, really, I did not care.

The whole team and Vera and Jenny and Andrea took me to the Charlottesville SPCA. Jenny held my hand and told me it was all right to get a new dog and that Someday was okay with it, too. I walked up and down the aisles looking at dogs in the cages. When I got to cage number forty-two, I saw a gaunt, skinny six-month old: a whippet Lab mix of sorts. She was lying in some of her own waste.

"She's on her second return to here." A worker had come up from behind. "Evidently she digs to beat the band and she's a barker, too."

"She seems so quiet," I said.

"Yeah. Well she's on her way out if you know what I mean. She's been here three weeks."

Jenny asked the lady if she would open the cage. I looked at Teeter and she smiled her smile at me. She whispered under her breath that I was dumb and then nudged me.

Andrea and Vera came from a few cages down. Vera put her hand to her forehead. "Jeez. That looks like Gracie-Mac. My old doggie I had years ago. I can't believe it."

"She looks like she needs a bath," Andrea said.

The cage door opened and I stood looking at the blond dog with almond eyes. She looked at me. I called for her. "Come here, sweetie," I said.

Tentatively and on all fours, the dog scratched toward me from the back of the cage. I let her sniff my hands and then was not sure for a moment. Then without notice, she put her head on my shoulder and licked my ear.

Everyone laughed.

I was sorry when my family died. I was very sad when Someday died. They all died too soon a death, to me. But when I died my bipolar death, when I lost my mind, my living family saw a place inside of me die and were scared I'd never come back. Much later, in a conversation with Vera and Andrea and Jenny, they would tell me this. They weren't sure if I'd make it out of the hospital. After all, I was determined to change the world by calling in all my saints, Christopher Reeve and assorted celebrities. I was certain that I had to endure the pain of humanity in the metaphors of paralysis, and child abuse, and murder as they'd come up. I thought that what I had endured was going to be enough evidence to God and Jesus and the whole world that my five-pound teeming brain with all of its dark and light could save it if someone would just read the womanifesto. Just read it. Just read it. Just read it.

I named my new dog Chopin because she was part of my own personal awakening. She slept with me on my first night back at Teeter's and my apartment and we began a new bond, a new life. I played guitar and sang her Someday's favorite goofy song that Teeter hated: "Sweet Surrender" by John Denver. We all three ate Froot Loops in the morning and giggled at its own contradiction. Teeter explained while painting her nails that her heaven was twenty-six miles down the road to Culpeper where her parents died. She spoke of it softly and I listened to her. Chopin cocked her ears a bit like Someday's every time Teeter said the word, radonkulous.

I was too embarrassed to return to basketball. I don't think Potter would have had me back anyway. A few players looked at me weird and Mandy Weaver became elusive, like some people become. I was sure she would fall in love with me and stick around. But, when you lose your mind and think it's the allegory for the world, sometimes people run away. She did. I never really saw much of her again.

With a red scarf wrapped around my neck, I drove Chopin and me home to Banff for the month off at Christmas. Andrea said I shouldn't drive all that way . . . but driving calmed me. I cracked the window and Chopin stuck her head out of it in the same way Someday had. She put her furry blond head on the edge of the window and regarded me from time to time to make sure I was still there. When we crossed bridges over most of the United States and part of Canada, I would glance at Chopin and think of my family and Someday.

My name is Piper Leigh Cliff. My brain is not tainted with a disease but gifted with it. It is not the allegory for the world. It will not cure paralysis, nor will it save the world from criminals. Instead, I know this for sure: my heart loves grandly—my soul feels grandly. Both my heart and soul have broken through and seen the realms of other places. It has seen the evil and the good. My small spirit has broken through. It is the larger breaking spirits, though, that change the world: like the spirit of John Kennedy, the spirit of Robert Kennedy, the spirit of Marilyn Monroe, the spirits of Christopher Reeve and Dana Reeve, of even the living spirits like Nelson Mandela—of course, the spirits of the saints, especially J of A.

Riding in my truck with my dog by my side is the best healing in the world. We are going home for my birthday and for Christmas. Watching her ears flapping in the wind while holding her paw in the palm of my hand—this is a miracle. A miracle, a miracle, a miracle.

And, now, this is what matters most in my world.

Acknowledgements

Special recognition and gratitude goes out to my sister, Mary Kathryn Perkinson, who is the smartest, funniest woman I know. This book would not have come about if she had not opened her home to me and let me live and breathe and write. I am the luckiest sister in the world to have her.

I found Sandy Rakowitz in beautiful Charlottesville, Virginia, this year. She has given me great joy. Here's to much more dancing and laughing and loving. You are a wonderful, gifted healer of people and animals—a true messenger of light for ones in need.

Terri Nelson came into my life and believes in me more than I do sometimes. She is a gifted writer who from time to time gives me just the right criticism and I run to make the changes. This book is better because of her.

A true honor was bestowed on me when my beautiful publisher, Linda Hill, asked Katherine Forrest to edit this book. I am still reeling from this. What a great editor! Thank you for nudging me in the right places and giving me wonderful, adroit feedback.

Then, of course, there is my dog, River. She passed her Delta Society test this past year and is a certified therapy dog. I love her more and more each day. She goes to visit people in schools, homes and hospitals and they pet her and love on her and she makes them feel more alive. Good girl.

Lastly, I'd like to say that mental illness in any form, whether it is bipolar disorder, schizophrenia, clinical depression, obsessive compulsive disorder—whatever one you want to name—these illnesses can be heartbreaking for the people who suffer from them as well as for the friends and family who witness from the sidelines. I'd like to thank, personally, all the people who stick by their mentally ill loved ones in the face of true darkness; but, please know, that there is hope.

To everyone who reads this—peace, strength, joy and abundant simplicity in your lives, always.

Publications from Spinsters Ink

**P.O. Box 242
Midway, Florida 32343
Phone: 800-301-6860
www.spinstersink.com**

ACROSS TIME by Linda Kay Silva. If you believe in soul mates, if you know you've had a past life, then join Jessie in the first of a series of adventures that takes her Across Time.

ISBN 978-1883523-91-6 $14.95

SELECTIVE MEMORY by Jennifer L. Jordan. A Kristin Ashe mystery. A classical pianist, who is experiencing profound memory loss after a near-fatal accident, hires private investigator Kristin Ashe to reconstruct her life in the months leading up to the crash.

ISBN 978-1-883523-88-6 $14.95

HARD TIMES by Blayne Cooper. Together, Kellie and Lorna navigate through an oppressive, hidden world where lines between right and wrong blur, sexual passion is forbidden but explosive, and love is the biggest risk of all.   ISBN 978-1-883523-90-9 $14.95

THE KIND OF GIRL I AM by Julia Watts. Spanning decades, *The Kind of Girl I Am* humorously depicts an extraordinary woman's experiences of triumph, heartbreak, friendship and forbidden love.

ISBN 978-1-883523-89-3 $14.95

PIPER'S SOMEDAY by Ruth Perkinson. It seemed as though life couldn't get any worse for feisty, young Piper Leigh Cliff and her three-legged dog, Someday.   ISBN 978-1-883523-87-9 $14.95

MERMAID by Michelene Esposito. When May unearths a box in her missing sister's closet she is taken on a journey through her mother's past that leads her not only to Kate but to the choices and compromises, emptiness and fullness, the beauty and jagged pain of love that all women must face.   ISBN 978-1-883523-85-5 $14.95

ASSISTED LIVING by Sheila Ortiz-Taylor. Violet March, an eighty-two-year-old resident of Casa de los Sueños, finally has the opportunity to put years of mystery reading to practical use. One by one her comrades, the Bingos, are dying. Is this natural attrition, or is there a sinister plot afoot?
ISBN 978-1-883523-84-2 $14.95

NIGHT DIVING by Michelene Esposito. *Night Diving* is both a young woman's coming-out story and a thirty-something coming-of-age journey that proves you can go home again.
ISBN 978-1-883523-52-7 $14.95

FURTHEST FROM THE GATE by Ann Roberts. *Furthest from the Gate* is a humorous chronicle of a woman's coming of age, her complicated relationship with her mother and the responsibilities to family that last a lifetime.   ISBN 978-1-883523-81-7 $14.95

EYES OF GRAY by Dani O'Connor. Grayson Thomas was the typical college senior with typical friends, a typical job and typical insecurities about her future. One Sunday morning, Gray's life became a little less typical, she saw a man clad in black, and started doubting her own sanity.
ISBN 978-1-883523-82-4 $14.95

ORDINARY FURIES by Linda Morgenstein. Tired of hiding, exhausted by her grief after her husband's death, Alexis Pope plunges into the refreshingly frantic world of restaurant resort cooking and dining in the funky chic town of Guerneville, California.
ISBN 978-1-883523-83-1 $14.95

A POEM FOR WHAT'S HER NAME by Dani O'Connor. Professor Dani O'Connor had pretty much resigned herself to the fact that there was no such thing as a complete woman. Then out of nowhere, along comes a woman who blows Dani's theory right out of the water.
ISBN 1-883523-78-8 $14.95

WOMEN'S STUDIES by Julia Watts. With humor and heart, *Women's Studies* follows one school year in the lives of three young women and shows that in college, one's extracurricular activities are often much more educational than what goes on in the classroom.
ISBN 1-883523-75-3 $14.95

DISORDERLY ATTACHMENTS by Jennifer L. Jordan. The fifth Kristin Ashe Mystery. Kris investigates whether a mansion someone wants to convert into condos is haunted.

ISBN 1-883523-74-5 $14.95

VERA'S STILL POINT by Ruth Perkinson. Vera is reminded of exactly what it is that she has been missing in life.

ISBN 1-883523-73-7 $14.95

OUTRAGEOUS by Sheila Ortiz-Taylor. Arden Benbow, a motorcycle-riding, lesbian Latina poet from LA is hired to teach poetry in a small liberal arts college in Northwest Florida.

ISBN 1-883523-72-9 $14.95

UNBREAKABLE by Blayne Cooper. The bonds of love and friendship can be as strong as steel. But are they unbreakable?

ISBN 1-883523-76-1 $14.95

ALL BETS OFF by Jaime Clevenger. Bette Lawrence is about to find out how hard life can be for someone of low society standing in the 1900s.

ISBN 1-883523-71-0 $14.95

UNBEARABLE LOSSES by Jennifer L. Jordan. The fourth Kristin Ashe Mystery. Two elderly sisters have hired Kris to discover who is pilfering from their award-winning holiday display.

ISBN 1-883523-68-0 $14.95

EXISTING SOLUTIONS by Jennifer L. Jordan. The second Kristin Ashe Mystery. When Kris is hired to find an activist's biological father, things get complicated when she finds herself falling for her client.

ISBN 1-883523-69-9 $14.95

A SAFE PLACE TO SLEEP by Jennifer L. Jordan. The first Kristin Ashe Mystery. Kris is approached by well-known lesbian Destiny Greaves with an unusual request. One that will lead Kris to hunt for her own missing childhood pieces.

ISBN 1-883523-70-2 $14.95